HERE
The Y

Paul Devine

The author reserves the right not to be responsible for the topicality, correctness, completeness or quality of the information provided. Liability claims regarding damage caused by the use of any information provided, including any kind of information which is incomplete or incorrect, will therefore be rejected.

Copyright © 2021 Paul Devine.
All rights reserved.

This book is for all of those affected by the Coronavirus Pandemic.

And for all Frontline Workers.

And for Linzi, my fellow hermit.

ABOUT THE AUTHOR

Paul Devine was the singer with Post-Punk band Siiiii for three years in the 1980's and a further nine between 2005 and 2014. The Devine Comedy, Paul's autobiography, was written during lockdown in 2020. He lives in Glastonbury, England with his wife Linzi, two grown men, roughly 170 bees and a Siberian Husky called Jack. Here Be Hermits, The Year of Covid is his second book.

BY THE SAME AUTHOR

2019

As I get ever more decrepit, I expect each year to be less notable than the one before. When my Mum and Dad were my age, as far as I'm aware, they went to work, drank tea in relative's houses on Sunday afternoons, and went on holiday once a year. Perhaps they lived in 'less interesting times', as the Confucian curse almost goes. Or perhaps, as I have been told, each generation experiences changes and events as powerfully as those who went before. They just don't talk about it much because they assume nobody's that interested.

2019 was another eyebrow-raising Year of Trump. The twin demons of this inhuman beast and Brexit seem to have brought out the very filthiest in humanity. It doesn't take much for the scum of the earth to slither from the depths of their moronic hatred and float to the surface. All it requires is something to disturb the silt enough to release the gases and up they pop, like sewer bubbles. I read somewhere that humanity has always suffered historical periods of welcoming psychopaths into powerful positions. Then humanity undergoes torment. Then humanity changes its ways. And once humanity has forgotten all about it, this dreadful cycle starts all over again. I pray that Trump is a blip. An aberration. A simple error. Also, the term 'Brexiteers' suggests something brave and swashbuckling. They're not brave or heroic or devil-may-care. They're idiots. How about 'Brexiters'? Or 'Twats'?

The hotel in Chesterfield I have been dreaming for years showed its dark side at last. I suspected it might happen. The usual narrative of these dreams is my riding a pushbike from Glastonbury to the hotel. Then I have a meal and a pleasant conversation with the woman who runs it. And then I wake up. Having never been to Chesterfield, it's only via dream-dialogue and road signs that I know it's in Chesterfield at all. The hotel is a Georgian or Regency three-storey building with bricks darkened by pollution and age. The top two floors contain the gilded hotel rooms, and the proprietor runs an off-licence on the more-modern-looking ground floor. On my recent visit I arrived by bike as usual, but booked myself into the hotel for the first ever time. Once I had made myself comfortable in my very baroque room, I enjoyed my meal. This time, though, I was aware of being observed by the stupid, corpselike portraits hanging all around the dining room where I was eating alone. Once dinner was finished, I retired to bed, where I heard someone talking outside my room. I rose and opened the door. A woman with no eyes or teeth or operational jaw stood in the corridor. She wore soil-stained Georgian clothing and said that she had been waiting for me for years. This woman beckoned me to the attic, which was up a narrow and dim stairway at the end of the hallway. All of my pets were there. Jack, Cloud, Mogg, childhood cats and rabbits. They were dead but moving. Shrunken. Mummified. Covered in unhealed wounds. My pets were screaming in terrible pain. The walls began to darken with black and green mould. As I inhaled the mould spores, I felt the tendrils of decay grow in my lungs and spread to my guts. And when I woke up, I thought I was dead.

Hair of various locations has been a bit of an issue this year. I bought a new electric shaver and, as usual, I took it out of the box, chucked the instructions, and started shearing away. On the first occasion of trimming my moustache, I gave myself a 'Reverse Hitler', in that the little bit under my nose was the only completely hairless part of my face. I also noticed, in about March, that my pubic hair has gone grey, but only at the sides. Down There now looks like the late Trevor Bolder from David Bowie's band's sideburns during their "Starman" era.

On the subject of horrors, I endured another sigmoidoscopy this year due to a cancer scare. The enema necessary for the procedure is now self-administered at home. The directions state: "Lay on the floor in a comfortable position. Put as much of the flexible tube into your bottom (anus) as you comfortably can, and gently squeeze the bag. If you feel any pressure, then stop. You may not use all of the liquid in the bag."

The tube disappeared almost completely. And I could have easily shoved another couple of bagfuls up there. Unbeknownst to me, my bottom can be described as 'roomy'. The subsequent sigmoidoscopy went as well as these things can. The NHS staff and I were talking about cauliflower rice and feeding salmon to dogs while I was having it done. The Entonox Gas & Air was incredible. Two unexpected bonuses were that there was hardly any agony this time around, and that I sound like Barry White on Gas & Air. I was amazed and a little nauseated when the consultant, one Mr Simeon Pew, leaned over me with a leery grin, prodded me just below my ribcage and said, "The camera's all the way up here you know!". It turned out that I had no signs of bowel cancer, which was a relief. When we got home, I changed out of my hospital slops and strolled into the living room looking like The Fonz, with my leather jacket collar turned up and my hair all a-flutter. I asked Linzi if she wanted to "go driving and parking up at the local make-out spot". She said no.

I carried on creating stones for Cloud Stone Art this year. Following 2018's triumph at the Glastonbury Frost Fayre I was keen to exhibit at the 2019 one. My house and garden, after work, was the site of a proper cottage industry. Something called Liquid Glass caught my eye in June, so I bought some. It is a two-part resin, and the idea, as I understood it, is that you mix the two parts together and then do whatever it is that you want to do with it. Whatever object it is that you are doing things with it to then has a crystal-clear and glass-like casing. This miracle liquid, I decided, would encase my largest works (Breughel, Bosch, some large Anatomical Studies and the Feathered Skull), within a transcendental carapace of transparent and glittering beauty. As with the beard trimmer, I didn't read the instructions. Every piece I used it on stuck hard to the cardboard I sat it on to dry. And I had to use a grinder to fetch it and the adhered cardboard off. Apart from looking terrible, I needed to remove the stuff because of the overpowering cabbage/petroleum chemical-spill stench it gave off. This resin, it became apparent on looking at the manual, is not designed for large objects. It is meant for small items to create an effect something like insects in amber. Armed with this new knowledge, I then chose to dip my stone Christmas decorations into this Liquid Glass and hung them inside the shed, on garden twine, from the ceiling, to dry. The resin dripped onto everything. My lawnmower. My garden tools. Several of my other almost completed pieces. Out came the grinder again. Because this stuff dries like granite. And it fucking stinks.

During the summer, our upstairs toilet started making foghorn noises, The Specials played The Glastonbury Extravaganza, and I went on a Low Carb food regime. The toilet eventually stopped its caterwauling, but not before expanding its musical repertoire to include the opening notes of the blues standard Stormy Weather. An engineer came to fix the issue and since his fine work, the toilet finishes its cistern refill with a powerful bang loud enough to be heard two doors away, especially at night. The Specials are the third best band I have ever seen (#1 Sex Pistols and #2 The Birthday Party) and, in the bright and grassy outdoor arena of Glastonbury Abbey in June, with some great friends and lots of booze, the experience was remarkable. Due to being massively overweight, though, I had to keep sitting down between prancing about to songs to catch my breath. And the realisation of how out-of-shape I had become then made me decide to lose some weight. I booked an appointment with my doctor. During the consultation my GP said, a little directly, "You're quite fat, Paul. Look at me!", and I looked at this lithe man who is about five years older than I am. "I don't eat carbohydrates", he said. "When you eat carbs, your body says 'Ooooh! Sugars!' and you get fat. Like you are." Then he gave me a printout of carb-avoiding food ideas. On getting this sheet of paper home, I decided there and then to start this discipline. Over three months I lost almost three stone. I got evangelical about it, as is usual, and sent out a whole swathe of "Low Carb Devine" emails, containing recipes and advice, to friends and family, whether they wanted them or not.

Autumn came around and Boris Johnson chickened out of a planned visit to Glastonbury. I drove past where this Trump-lite berk was due to have graced us with his presence. I doubt he'd have got in for all the protestors.

It was at about this point that we started to notice infuriating Just Eat advertisements on the TV. "Did somebody say... Just Eat?" Then "Just Eat" started emailing me for no reason. I finally responded to these emails as follows:

"As nobody in this house has ever "*said Just Eat*" and are very unlikely to, and as you keep sending me your emails, just so you know, I'll be ordering Fuck All with a side of Fuck Off.'"

October meant that Frost Fayre was just around the corner. Brigid at Beckets Inn on the High Street let me take over the large Carriage Bar to trial my Cloud Stone Art stall one evening. It looked fabulous, especially with the new bubble-lights, and even more especially after a couple of pints. The Frost Fayre itself was great. We met some splendid people and I sold most of my stock. We had the obligatory several pints in Beckets Inn afterwards.

There was also a Christmas video to film and record. This year I chose John Paul Young's "Love Is in The Air". While not necessarily festive, I have always liked the song's upbeat and optimistic feel. I filmed some person-sized Nutcracker Soldiers at TK Maxx. And Linzi filmed me on the Santa Train at Cadbury Garden Centre. Before the procession on Carnival Night, for further footage, I put on my sister's huge 1970's sunglasses and a Stetson wrapped in tinsel and filmed myself miming to the song while walking back and forth beside the bright illuminations. I imagine the Carnival Clubs assumed I was just another Glastonbury weirdo. When I came to edit the video, I forgot all about the Nutcracker Soldiers and the Santa Train. I'll use them next year. If I remember.

The Tories won yet another inexplicable landslide in the General Election in December. I have a theory. Anyone who cannot extricate a Tesco shopping trolley from the one in front without resorting to violence forfeits the right to vote. All you need to do is gently lift the leg-hole-closure and your trolley slides out. It's obvious after a few seconds of observation but I spend a lot of time sitting outside Tescos, and seeing anyone manage it is a rarity. The Great British Public have spoken. Again. God help us. Again.

I opened my pair-of-slippers Christmas present from my Mum early this year, so I now have Indoor Slippers and Outdoor Slippers. As the two pairs are similar colours though, I have had to stick adhesive red FRAGILE tape on the outdoor pair.

Jack started having some throat and stomach issues, so we've started giving him live yoghurt. It might be down to the amount of soil he keeps eating. And I decided in November that I had lost enough weight to start eating normally again. Obviously, especially as we've just had Christmas, I'm getting fat again.

Christmas was lovely, as usual. The Antonio Carluccio meal that Linzi creates every year took eight hours to make again, meaning we were all ready for bed after the Christmas pudding. A few days after Christmas, I needed something from the garden shed, and because the Christmas Tree is always put up in front of the back door, I had to scale the 6ft fence to the side of the house to get into the back. I got stuck, Outdoor Slippers flailing about, until a neighbour helped me to get back down. I have never felt so middle aged.

So here we go on another spin around the Sun. It's weird, entering the twenties. My Dad was born in the twenties. It makes me feel a little uncoupled. I hope this year is as uneventful as possible.

JANUARY 2020

Wednesday January 1st (Jack's Birthday)

Happy 12th Birthday to Jack, my lovely, big, demanding, infuriating, soppy, daft, brilliant, irreplaceable Husky. We took him to the Bird Reserve at Ham Wall as a birthday treat. They've now got a viewing area near the sewage treatment area, which they've arranged like a little cottage garden with bird feeders and beehouses. You look through holes in the wicker fence to see what's going on, without what's going on seeing you watching them. There were an amazing number and variety of birds. Blue tits, great tits, coal tits, wood pigeons, blackbirds, thrushes, goldfinches. We saw our first reed bunting. There was a large rat at large as well, who kept scuttling out of the undergrowth and pinching the food the birds were dropping out of their beaks. We could have watched all day. It was incredibly cathartic. Jack will have to wait until the chippy is frying again next week to get his traditional Large Birthday Haddock and Chips. Which means I'll have to wait as well. Bugger.

Thursday January 2nd

My bloody CPAP Mask kept unplugging itself overnight and the air-pipe was blowing about all over the bed like an unsupervised hosepipe. I hardly got any sleep. Linzi had a rubbish night because, according to her, it's like sleeping in an ice storm. She's grumpy. I'm grumpy.

Early night tonight because I kept getting told off for being a miserable bastard.

Saturday January 4th

I start work again on Monday. How the hell did that happen? So we're going to finish Christmas the way we started it a lifetime ago, by having Flaming Sambuccas. I'm starting to feel a bit disinterested in Cloud Stone Art.

Sunday January 5th

Christ Alive I must watch that syrupy aniseed crap. It's worse than bloody Pernod. I spent today feeling like I'd been dug up. Adding to my Flaming Sambucca-pain, someone posted Joy Division's 'Atmosphere' on Facebook this morning. I responded with "Personally I prefer the Russ Abbott version" and now I can't get the bloody thing out of my head. We've got an appointment at the vet with Jack on Monday. He still has an upset stomach and keeps coughing.

Monday January 6th (Epiphany)

Last night Linzi told me that I'm 'like Mighty Joe Young' in bed. Today she told me that the Mighty Joe Young thing was about the noise and the smell.

Tuesday January 7th

Jack went to the local vets, where Violet the Vet took some bloods. He had to be muzzled because we forgot to take his usual Distraction Carrot. Fingers crossed he's just eaten another frog or some more compost or something.

Thursday January 9th

We have been advised that Jack almost certainly has a lymphoma-type cancer. The blood results put his calcium levels at extremely high. Violet the Vet has consulted two local specialists who concur with her. So now we start the dog-with-cancer process once more, using the same specialist in Wellington, Noelle, who looked after Cloud when she was poorly. I'm heartbroken. Jack is insured. He's also twelve, which is a grand age for a Husky. The situation is markedly different. The pain, however, is not.

Saturday January 11th

I got heroically and despairingly drunk yesterday evening. This morning's hangover was equally epic. I sobbed on the front path last night when I took Jack for his nightly parade around the block, because it might be one of the last times I get to do it. My little lad. I received an email yesterday with an appointment day (Tuesday) for him at the Specialist Vet. I can't believe we're in this situation again.

Tuesday January 14th

We hope, hope, hope!! Noelle the Specialist Vet examined Jack and played about with him in her room for a while. She then said in her methodical way that she would be *very* surprised if he has a lymphoma because of how lively he is and how much he's eating. She said that it's far more likely to be an overactive adrenal gland, and if that is the case it just needs whipping out. Then she marched him off to muzzle him and take bloods for a hormonal study and to check his calcium level. The results showed that his calcium is the same as last week. With a lymphoma she would have expected a considerable increase. We find out in one to two weeks for certain. We're not out of the firing-line yet, but it looks like we might have dodged a bullet with the boy! I'm driving back to East Anglia for my monthly work meeting tomorrow.

Wednesday January 15th

I am at my childhood home in East Anglia for tomorrow's meeting. I always stay here so I get to see my mother and eat her dinners and it's only ten miles to Head Office. As usual me and my Mum had a game of Scrabble. Why can I still not use certain words when playing Scrabble with her? Tonight I had LABIA, COME and BREASTS and I just couldn't do it.

Thursday January 16th

Just as I had pulled onto the A303 after the meeting yesterday, there was a tremendous THUD from the back of the car. I looked round to make sure the back door was still on and then manoeuvred the wing mirror to see if the tyres were still inflated, which they were. When I got back home, I got the torch out. There's a two-foot wide, circular, greyish, splat on the rear right-hand side of the car.

Either:

1. Someone who eats newspapers vomited semi-digested Papier-mâché onto my car.

2. An irate and spiteful farmer catapulted a dead piglet at me.

3. I sideswiped an unsuspecting and recently exorcised poltergeist.

4. The USS Enterprise transported someone into North Somerset by accident.

Jack seems fine, thank god. We're just waiting for the call from Noelle.

Friday January 17th

Matt, the Commercial Director, is coming down next Wednesday 'to spend a couple of days in my homeworking environment'. He may not realise that my homeworking environment is beneath a very hairy man's bunk-bed and that I have to remove stray pubic hairs and bogies from my desk most mornings.

Saturday January 18th

I just found this on my camera roll. Apparently I did it last night. I have absolutely no recollection. Not a sausage.

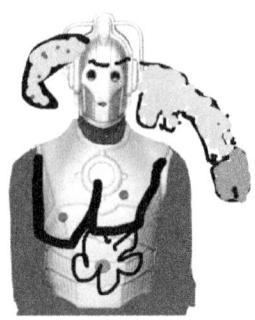

Sunday January 19th

2020's New Year message from TV advertisers seems to be: "You'll need to book a holiday once you've bought a sofa in our sale you fat bastards!"

Monday January 20th

Apparently, eels and other fish in the River Thames are displaying unnatural behaviours due to the huge quantities of high-quality cocaine going down London's toilets. I wonder if I could persuade anyone to come into the coke-panning business with me? A pint of Thames piss, correctly treated, could get us £150 worth of Bermondsey Marching Sludge.

Tuesday January 21st

Noelle called today. Jack is booked in for his ultrasound and potential operation with a Gland Expert at the Specialist Vets at 9am tomorrow. I made a stone for her at the weekend with the dogs on it, to thank her for all of her help with both Cloud and Jack.

Wednesday January 22nd

We met the Gland Expert. He is a tall and awkward blond man called Harvey with an almost inaudible voice and an impenetrable accent from somewhere or other. He explained the procedure to us and, after we had said our goodbyes, he took Jack into the surgery area. When we got in the car to come home, Linzi turned to me and asked, "Did you understand anything that man was saying?"

"Not a word" I replied. So I called Noelle when we got home to find out what he'd told us. They already know it isn't a cancer, thank God. It is, as Noelle thought, a couple of glands that need to be removed. This procedure costs a fortune though. I called my insurers and, who'd have guessed, they 'don't cover everything'. We are therefore going to have to prostrate ourselves once again before the good and caring folk of Punk/Post Punk/Goth Facebook once more via a GoFundMe fundraiser.

Thankfully, Matt's visit here is indefinitely postponed, so I won't have to watch him surreptitiously gathering pubis for his little nest at the Travelodge.

Thursday January 23rd

Our fundraiser reached target within three hours of going live. Bless Them All!! Jack will be in the Specialist Vets for up to five nights though. This is going to be tough.

Saturday January 25th (Burns Night)

Harvey called me during the procedure. He said something about a cannula and legs or something, and something about veins. After the call I rang Noelle for a translation. Harvey, it seems, carried out the operation successfully. And Jack is now back with Noelle, who is keeping him under observation for a couple of nights. He is exactly 33.4 miles away and I miss him.

We had a sad haggis.

Sunday January 26th

Noelle called us at 8am this morning asking us if we could visit Jack. We drove the 33.4 miles early this afternoon. Although he has only been away for four nights, he came out of the back looking and behaving like a completely different dog. To begin with he didn't recognise us. He was agitated. He skittered about in Noelle's room and almost fell over a few times. The duty veterinary nurse suggested we take him outside, which we did. He still seemed confused and wary and sad. I left him with Linzi and filled a bowl full of water from the tap in the waiting room toilet. Once he smelled the water, Jack drank and drank. I ran another bowl, and he drank that one too. Such a thirsty animal. I don't for a moment think he was deprived of water to drink. I just don't believe he wanted it if we weren't with him. The duty nurse came out and watched us with him. She asked us to stay where we were, and then she telephoned Noelle. Thankfully, this most wonderful of vets said that we should take him home with us there and then. We signed his release form and paid (again, I love my people), and we brought him home. Once he was where he belonged, he fell asleep on his bed for hours and hours, silently healing. I left the stone I made for Noelle with the nurse at the vets. I hope she likes it.

Monday January 27th

Jack was bouncing about all over the house today. The area where he had his glands removed looks startling and bare, being shaved and stitched, but he ate like a horse and is allowed (temporarily it seems) to sleep on the sofa next to me. I need to collect some of his wee for Violet the Vet to check his calcium levels next week. Can't wait.

The dreary man-child that is Matt Hancock made a statement in Parliament today about a virus in Asia. It's the first I've heard about it. All UK citizens in China are going to be flown home as a matter of urgency.

Tuesday January 28th

I had my first 10-weekly Testosterone injection of the year today. My levels are described as dangerously low and have been for years. Siiiii's bassist, Ange, reckons I used it all up in the eighties, trawling the clubs of Sheffield It's a huge amount of fluid, so Nurse Helen always warms it in a dish of hot water to loosen it prior to pumping this huge, golf-ball-sized lump of medicine into my arse. Nurse Helen is lovely and the procedure is always painless with her. She invades your personal space a bit though. And I keep thinking she's about to pounce.

Wednesday January 29th

British Airways have suspended flights to mainland China! I didn't see that coming, especially as the Tories and their corporate gang are emulating the grimy Trump by making the acquisition of money the sole reason for drawing breath.

I have come to the decision that, after Noelle's piece, I am not making further Cloud Stone Art pieces. I think I did her proud. I hope so anyway.

Friday January 31ˢᵗ (British Self-Immolation Day)

I had another shower today because it's Brexit Day, and it makes me feel filthy. I washed my hair as well. Just to be sure.

Apparently it's called Coronavirus, and a couple of Brits have been diagnosed with it.

FEBRUARY 2020

Saturday February 1st

jumped out of my skin this afternoon thinking someone was scowling through the kitchen window at me. It was a Sky TV van parked outside the house with a massive picture of Andre Rieu on the side.

Sunday February 2nd

Some ITV phone-in competition broadcast a trailer this morning. A woman who had previously won said that she didn't believe she'd won, and her husband didn't believe she'd won either. Her parents didn't believe she'd won. And neither did her kids, her sisters or any of her work colleagues. She's patently a habitual bloody liar.

Tuesday February 4th

Jack slept for hours last night. He didn't eat anything apart from some cheese with his vitamin D3 in it. This morning he had a poached salmon fillet, half a chicken fillet, some yoghurt and three dried meat treats. I took his urine calcium vials to Violet the Vet down the road, and he had a quick walk round their car park afterwards. He really can't settle if we're out of the room. And he keeps sitting as close to us as possible. And on us, if a handy lap or two is available. I'm concerned about his behaviour. And it's apparently bad form to wipe your fingers on him after eating a particularly anarchic sausage and tomato sandwich.

Thursday February 6th

We just caught the news, and apparently a third person in the country has got the Coronavirus.

I have devised a tasty lunchtime menu for the heavily mooted Wetherspoons/Trump USA food supply deal.

Milwaukee Tinned 'Pot Luck' Chapped Nuggets
Yankee Cowboy Leg o'Sumthin'
Maine-Style Aquatic Thing
'Home on the Range' Pig's Dick
Tennessee Granny McCloud's Creamy Strained Fluid
Greyish Detroit Clumps in Syrup
Porky Scrapings Arkansas
'Finest' Sizzling Pallid Iowa Tissue
New York Basket-au-Shit

Saturday February 8th

"We're here to help." simpers that wretched woman on the new 'caring' Injury Lawyers 4U ad, while the rest of them stand about close to tears. I preferred it when they looked like they wanted to kick your teeth in.

Monday February 10th

We had a conversation after work today about cannibalism and the Tesco horsemeat scandal a few years ago. We're both vegetarians, and Linzi says she'd never eat human or horse. I said I'd eat human if I could choose the victim, but I wouldn't eat horse. I'd have to think about centaur.

Wednesday February 12th

Harvey the Gland Specialist rang and gave us Jack's test results. I thanked him, and then phoned Noelle so I could find out what they were. His calcium is a bit high, when it should be a bit low. So she says to reduce his vitamin D3 by three quarters. There goes most of his cheese ration! We will take him for further bloods on Monday at the local vets.

Thursday February 13th

According to some fashionista on Radio 4 this morning, eyebrows are back in. Thank God for that! I've hardly dared show my out-of-date upper face in public for years. Although I did buy a hat so I could look out of the window.

Jack's appointment went well. We took a Distraction Carrot for him, but the veterinary staff still had to throw a duvet over him to stop him twatting about with his teeth. Violet the Vet eventually managed to get some bloods. She remarked at what a lively boy he is. She doesn't know the half of it. Because of this situation, Linzi and I later discussed what pet we should get that would outlive us and we somehow decided on an oyster.

Friday February 14th (Valentine's Day)

Recreational mind-altering drugs (alcohol, actual drugs etc) would be unnecessary if the world wasn't so fucking ghastly.

You wake up in the morning at Zero. But by 3pm you've reached the magic Ten on the "I-Just-Can't-Fucking-Bear It-Omiter".

Wake Up. Yawn. Stretch. Get up.--- **0**
Put News on TV. People killing each other for no reason--- **2**
Start Work. Immediately have to deal with halfwits--- **3**
Lunchtime. Walk Jack. Negotiate the usual dog shit and broken glass obstacle course--- **4**
Drive Back Home. Boy/girl racers driving like toddlers --- **5**

DINGDINGDINGDING!! Where's The Bastard Gin??

We had a Valentine's Curry tonight. Because nothing says Romance like explosive flatulence.

Saturday February 15th

Violet the Vet called today following Jack's blood test, and his calcium levels are now completely within the normal range. It looks like he's better! I posted enormous and effusive thanks to everyone who helped during his little fundraiser. We are incredibly happy!

Sunday February 16th

On a whim I made some peanut butter and honey oat biscuits tonight. They are probably the best thing I have ever baked, not that that's much of a barometer of quality. But everyone liked them. I am a Star Baker!

Monday February 17th

There were three of the oat biscuits left this morning, so I brought them into the living room to dunk into my tea for breakfast. I went into the kitchen to get the tea. Came back to this.

Thursday February 20th

Fun With ADHD!

Got into the shower.
The water came out in a pathetic dribble.
Realised the head was a bit clogged up with limescale.
Got out.
Looked on the bathroom shelf.
Found a sinister-looking bottle of Domestos with the word 'limescale' on it.

Took the shower head off.
Filled it up with the Domestos.
Left it for ten minutes.
Rinsed it out.
Got back into shower

Got back out after about a minute because it felt like my skin was ablaze.

Noticed that the first and largest instruction on the bottle, which was called Domestos Ultra Toilet Destroyer or something, was "Wear Suitable Gloves". The second was "Avoid Contact With Skin".

Monday February 24th

Looking forward to watching everyone in the house scarfing down wet flour tomorrow. Mmmmm. Pancakes. What a load of old crap. At least I won't be here.

Tuesday February 25th (St Pancake's Day)

I'm in East Anglia at my Mum's for the monthly meeting tomorrow.

Scrabble Failures: FLAPS. ERECT. QUIM (triple word!!).

Wednesday February 26th

Someone found a gastric worm in one of the toilets at work last week, and personal cleanliness signs have appeared everywhere. I didn't enquire too deeply into this turn of events but the questions Who? and How? keep popping into my mind.

When I got home, I emailed my Mum and asked her how she makes the gravy on the vegetarian roasts she cooks taste so brilliant. She replied, "I just use the fat and juice from meat and good old Bisto!"

Friday February 28th

The sun came out for ten minutes last week, allowing us to actually see things. And, ever since, we've been debating whether to keep paying our window cleaner £10 a time to throw filthy water about all over the place.

Worrying news about a Coronavirus outbreak in Scotland. The sportswear company, Nike, held a massive conference there and a lot of delegates have come down with it. I'm guessing that they weren't all from Scotland, and so they'll have all hopped on planes and gone back to Christ knows where. We've looked about and we can't even find out what the symptoms are, but allegedly it's incurable. Johnson's sage advice is to wash our hands for the amount of time it takes to sing Happy Birthday.

It has also come to light that Johnson missed not one but five COBRA (Cabinet Office Briefing Rooms... I don't know about the 'A') emergency meetings regarding COVID-19 a few weeks back, and then buggered off on holiday to The Caribbean.

Saturday February 29th

While Johnson is currently relaxing at his country manor near Oxford, the NHS said today that it faces a nightmarish PPE (Personal Protective Equipment... vital to stop the COVID-19 virus infecting NHS staff) shortage. Stockpiles of PPE have dwindled or expired after years of Tory austerity cuts.

And someone from the UK has died. On a cruise ship. Imagine being on board a ship and some new virus running wild. It is a horror story. And some people who came back from an Italian skiing- holiday have got it too. It's escalating quickly. We're beginning to realise that this thing is serious.

MARCH 2020

Sunday March 1st (St David's Day)

We have had a couple of pints at Beckets Inn nearly every Sunday afternoon for over ten years. On Sundays, as long as one of the regulars who I swear uses a hoover hasn't already been in and eaten the lot, there are free bar snacks to enjoy. Crisps, olives, pickled onions, cheese biscuits, crackers, mature local cheddar. All perfect with a pint! We went in today and I took our usual drinks to our usual table. Then I went back to the bar and filled my hands with various snack-bowl sweetmeats. Linzi glared at me when I sat back down and said, "There's that virus in Britain now you know!" I already had the haul in my grasp, so I thought about it, said "Nah!", and ate everything. But Linzi kept looking at me, and it became apparent that any further communal snacking in the pub would be a bad idea. The few meagre pleasures I can still enjoy at my age are being eroded by the day. I am bereft!

Monday March 2nd

A hearty round of applause today. Johnson attended his first COBRA meeting! His Mum wrote him a sick note for the ones he missed saying he had nits.

Sadly though, he declined an opportunity to join a European PPE scheme. Johnson's own scientists said that over half a million UK citizens could die if COVID-19 is not addressed properly. And meanwhile Johnson told us that we are, and I quote, "Very, very well prepared." I think I can see the way this thing is going to play out.

In brighter news, I walked into the kitchen to refresh my G&T this evening. Linzi was at the sink. She suddenly turned around with her Marigolds on, roared "PHROAAAAAAOOOOOR", and made as if to punch me in the bollocks. The noise was enough to bring the dog into the room. I needed a sit down outside afterwards because I very nearly shat myself.

Tuesday March 3rd

Today, Government scientists and other experts urged the Government to advise the Great British Public not to shake hands because of the potential of spreading the virus. Johnson was shaking the hands of Coronavirus patients.

Thursday March 5th

We've had our first Coronavirus death within the UK. As a country we have now progressed from something called the "Containment" Phase to something else called the "Delay" Phase. The Government has also published their action plan for dealing with COVID-19, as Coronavirus is now apparently called. The predicted scenarios go from a few people having a mild cough to a severe, prolonged and potentially civilisation-destroying pandemic. Comforting to know that our leaders have a clue what's going on.

Meanwhile, in Trumpton, the idiot has simultaneously told people who are sick with the virus to go to work and not to go to work. I'd suggest that this is the exact point where, globally, people suspend gathering in large numbers. Apart from Trump and his supporters. They need to keep having those rallies. More if possible. In more confined spaces. With no ventilation.

Friday March 6th

We were just starting to watch a Star Trek movie tonight when I glanced at Linzi. She suddenly covered her face with her hand and gaped at the wall behind me in horror. I jumped out of my bloody skin, ("What is it? Is it a hornet?? What the fuck Linz???") and only realised that there was nothing there when she started laughing. I needed a sit down outside afterwards because I very nearly shat myself.

Sunday March 8th

The third UK COVID-19 death was reported today. This one was in Manchester. We've decided, until someone not employed by the Tories tells us otherwise, that we're not going anywhere or seeing anyone. I'm fat and I'm allergic to everything and have Ulcerative Colitis. Linzi's fat and has asthma. It sounds like it would probably kill us both or at least have a bloody good try. Some new neighbours are moving in over the road. I just heard Coldplay coming from the house. It's the first time anyone's been off my Christmas card list before they're even on it.

A young Asian man called Jonathan Mok was attacked in London a few days ago. He was kicked senseless by some British men who were yelling "'We don't want your Coronavirus in our country!" Not that it makes any difference to this disgusting scenario, but Jonathon is from Singapore.

Did I imagine that the loon in the Whitehouse called COVID-19 "a Democrat Lie" yesterday? And did I imagine that that sausage dog who won Crufts celebrated by having a massive shit in the middle of the arena on its Victory Lap?

Tuesday March 10th

Ireland announced today that all St Patrick's day parades are cancelled this year due to the burgeoning COVID-19 pandemic. The UK Government said that there is "no rationale" for cancelling large sports events. Obviously, after "Delay" and "Contain", we have the "Gormless" Phase.

Wednesday March 11th

Continuing the theme, today saw 3,000 Atletico Madrid fans fly into Liverpool for a game of football.

Thursday March 12th

Happy Birthday to Me! Fifty-six years old. How the hell did that happen? The latest from the Government is that anyone with a bad cough should stay indoors for seven days. We went to Tesco for wine, gin and a treat for tomorrow, for one doesn't celebrate on a work night, and I saw some packets of River Cobbler in the frozen fish aisle. It has never struck me as a very appetising name for an eating fish. You say "River Cobbler". I hear "Swamp Bollock".

Friday March 13th

You hear people say that they can't believe their eyes quite frequently. But today I genuinely questioned what I was seeing. If it is obvious to us that now is exactly the moment to grow up, be sensible and think about your own health and that of others, then what the hell are a quarter-of-a-million people doing at the Cheltenham Races? It would be churlish of me to predict a deluge of COVID-19 cases following this circus, but I'm doing just that.

I also investigated Trump's work during what looks like a coming apocalypse today, as he has just declared a National Emergency. After weeks of lying and laughing COVID-19 off, much to the joy of his repugnant fanbase, he is taking no responsibility for anything. Has anyone told him it wasn't a game of charades and that he is, actually, the President?

The FA suspended the Premier League today because they could get no advice or guidance from the Government. And the UK was once more invited to join a European scheme for the joint purchase of ventilators, which are vital for people in ICU's (Intensive Care Units) with COVID-19. The UK Government said no. And Johnson upped the ante by lifting restrictions for people arriving in Britain from COVID-19 hot spots around the world.

Birthday Santa was kind today. My Mum bought me six months-worth of wild bird feed. And Linzi gave me a litre of Greenalls Wild Berry Gin, "The Mirror & The Light" by Hilary Mantel and a T Shirt with a bee on it. I got some cards too.

Saturday March 14th

Seventeen years ago, at about this time of year, I came upon a tiny, blue, featherless baby bird in my garden. I picked it up. It was freezing cold and utterly still. I assumed it was dead. Obviously, it had fallen from its nest. I almost put in in the dustbin, but something made me cup the little body in my hands and gently blow on it. After a little while it began to move very slightly. As I continued to warm the little bird it began to move a little more regularly.

A lady called Sally lived a few doors away, and Sally took in animal waifs and strays. I took the little bird, still in my hands, to her house. She took it in, saying it was so tiny that she fully expected it to die. She prepared a warm box for it anyway.

Some weeks later, Sally turned up at my door with her camcorder. She played me a movie she had taken. Her husband was in their garden holding the box. He smiled at the camera and then opened the lid A perfect, beautiful male blackbird put his head over the edge of the box, looked around, and then flew into the bold, blue, cloudless sky.

Sunday March 15th

We went to Tesco for supplies as we often do on a Sunday. We usually go before the pub, but it we're not going to the pub anymore. Half the shelves were bare. Pasta? No. Rice? No. Toilet paper? God no! The corner shop had a few rolls left. We usually use Cushelle. I don't know what the hell this stuff is, but it's about 60 grit. We have decided that, while we aren't selfish enough to stockpile, we're also aware enough of the intellect of the average Brit to get just that little bit extra per shop.

A couple of days ago, an Imperial College London study found that the Government's current COVID-19 plan is likely to kill half a million people.

Monday March 16th

Johnson said today that everyone must stop all non-essential contact and travel. We've been avoiding other people for weeks. Years in my case. He also advised people not to use pubs. But they're allowed to stay open. That's like giving someone a bike and telling them they can't ride it. Johnson had some humorous japing fun today too, during a conference call with a businessman pal. He joshed that the push to build more life-saving ventilators for potentially-dying COVID-19 victims should be called "Operation Last Gasp".

One of our neighbours was firebombed tonight. It was like Line of Duty! There were police cars, fire engines and ambulances everywhere, and a forensic team has just turned up. I have never seen so many of the people who live on this road standing about in the dark in so many stages of undress. All snouting around and gossiping. Me included.

Tuesday March 17th (St Patrick's Day)

We had a Skype conference at work today, and our monthly meetings are now suspended until we know the impact this virus is going to have. Although every cell in my body hates driving, I'm going to miss seeing my Mum every month. And eating her food. And I'm going to miss seeing my colleagues if I'm honest.

We're now heading for one hundred COVID-19 deaths and over 1,500 COVID-19 cases. The Government have advised against large public gatherings, but hey, if the cash is still rolling in! The loathsome Trump went on record today saying, "I've felt it was a pandemic long before it was called a pandemic. I've always viewed it as very serious."

There were around two-thirds fewer cars on the main Wells Road when I took Jack for a walk tonight. Quite unsettling. I used to close the bedroom windows to shut out all the noise. I've begun opening them just to hear some.

Wednesday March 18th

It's really cracking off now. Bloody hell. I have always believed that I would live through something world changing. I always assumed it would be an asteroid impact for some reason. We have rapidly exceeded one hundred COVID-19 deaths here. Schools, colleges and Universities have to close on March 20th. Apart from for Key Workers' and vulnerable schoolchildren. The value of the Pound has plummeted as well. Being dyscalculic I'm not totally sure what this means, but I imagine it's bad. The 50th Glastonbury Festival has been cancelled as well.

We tried Wotsits in Heinz Tomato Soup today. I suspect that this will be a unique experiment.

Thursday March 19th

The current Government apparently needs a slogan. Like 'Take Back Control'. The origin of the word 'slogan' is the Gaelic **sluagh**, which is a combination or 'army' and 'cry'. Our slogan is '"Stay home. Protect the NHS. Save lives."

Much as I did just after the foul Trump was elected and was in full spate, I am now checking the news before I get up every day. And Good God Almighty! The Government have decided that COVID-19 is no longer a 'high consequence infectious disease'. I'm racking my brain here to figure out what is behind this extraordinary statement. But no. Alas and alack I cannot solve the quandary.

Elderly hospital patients with COVID-19 are now being returned to care homes without any testing, to free up hospital space.

I'm considering keeping a log in this diary of all the random stuff that washes up on our lawn every day. Today's treasures: 1 Revels bag. 1 Benson & Hedges fag packet. 1 beige plastic letter H. 1 piece of black foam rubber. 1 Kellogg's Squares wrapper. 1 cat shit. 1 Greggs The Bakers bag.

Friday March 20th (March Equinox)

I've decided that T Rexes looked much better in the 1970's when they stood bolt upright like a fat bloke with a massive head and a tail, instead of the stupid, modern 'scientifically accurate' way they look now.

According to Johnson, the NHS PPE shortage has been "sorted".

Sunday March 22nd (Mothering Sunday)

I cooked everything and honoured Linzi like the Queen of Sheba she is today, and I spoke to my mother for Mother's Day.

Brigid at Beckets Inn had a beer takeaway this afternoon. She asked people to bring appropriate containers for the beer.

On the way home we noticed that a few windows are sporting rainbow pictures. They look like children's paintings.

Monday March 23rd

People are still emptying the supermarket shelves. The stupid, selfish bastards. I heard today that all of the major British grocers (Tesco, Aldi, Sainsbury's etc) are collectively recruiting over 30,000 staff to cope with the added pressure this virus may cause. I hope they'll be armed. The Government have said that "tougher measures" will be introduced if people don't follow social distancing rules. These rules are to stay two metres apart and to avoid gatherings (apart from enormous Government-recommended gatherings like The Cheltenham Festival, naturally) and it's actually pretty easy. Just grow up and think about someone other than yourselves. However, as this is totally dependent upon peoples' behaviour, I predict that the UK is a maximum of 24 hours from a total lockdown.

Well done Great British Public. You brainless, self-obsessed shower of shite.

Meanwhile in the Trump Swamp, a young girl called Yuanyuan Zhu was walking to a gym in San Francisco earlier in the month when some white man started yelling at her at a crossing. Zhu tried to keep away from this person but couldn't because there was not sufficient space. This man continued to glare and shout at her about 'the China virus' and then, when the crossing lights changed, he profusely spat at her.

Tuesday March 24th

LOCKDOWN! Or is it? I saw some footage shot in France a few days ago. A siren went off. Suddenly the streets were deserted. I can't see that sort of thing happening here, what with Churchill and that.

These are the rules as I understand them. We're only allowed to leave our houses for limited reasons. These reasons are food shopping, exercising once a day and for medical reasons. Also, and here's the clincher… travelling for work if absolutely necessary. That's most people then. Or at least those folks who don't fly a desk for a living like me. Therefore Blue Collar Workers are immediately expendable, because "if you have to travel to work… just get on with it you workshy oiks." Also, weddings are banned. And meetings of more than two people are now illegal. Funerals are still allowed though, with limited attendance. This is, sadly, just as well.

This new pass involved a couple of edgy conversations at my workplace. The main topic being "How can I do my job when nobody is allowed into other people's workplaces?" The mantra, after all, is still: Stay Home. Protect Lives. Save The NHS.

Why can't *everyone* stay at home though? Just for a while? Apart from food and other vital manufacturers, who could introduce reliable Track & Trace for their employees and make certain their employees are safe? But no. Building luxury condos and houses can't be delayed by something as trivial as a Global Pandemic. And, I believe, this will be the Achilles Heel of every Capitalist Government who look upon their populations with contempt. Either way, regardless of what any politicians spout, we're isolating and distancing until there's a proven vaccine. We are now hermits. For everyone's sakes.

Wednesday March 25th

I made us a lovely cheese and tomato sandwich for lunch. We both declared that the tomatoes were particularly tasty. San Marzano or something. I chewed one up to separate the seeds, spat some into a seed tray on a windowsill and poked them into the compost with a finger. Might work.

And Prince Charles has COVID-19. Our lives are becoming more like a disaster movie every day.

Thursday March 26th

At 8pm this evening, on the day that the new lockdown measures came into force, we did our first Clap for Carers. Most of our neighbours popped out. I was a bit late out of the door and Ray over the way tapped his watch. Those rainbow paintings we saw (they're all over the place now) are for the NHS as well. This show of appreciation was heart-warming and bizarre at the same time.

It occurred to me afterwards that, if Robert Winston is correct, and female human lips are brightly coloured to mimic an aroused vulva - and if women spend £millions a year on lipstick and similar products to subconsciously enhance this effect - why are mine such a lush and vivid shade of ripe pomegranate?

Friday March 27th

I was outside in the garden early tonight having a few drinks and talking to Stuart next door about viruses and gardening. When it started to get dark, we both went indoors. I was watching something on the TV when Stuart shouted, "Paul… come and look at this!"

Stuart was standing at the top of his garden and I joined him on my side of the garden fence. In the clear, dark sky was a moving row of lights, all travelling in the same direction and at the same speed. They disappeared, one by one, as they reached a point directly above us. "What the hell's that?" I whispered. "God knows." he replied. I called Linzi outside and we watched these strange little stars journey silently across the Somerset sky and wink out one by one. Stuart's wife, Carol came out to watch. We all stood, gazing at this endless parade of bright points, quietly wondering whether they could be military? or planes? If anything at all chronicled the surrealism of life at that moment, this was it. We ruled out everything they might have been. And, in my mind, the conclusion was either covert activity from some world power, or some unknown intelligence. These were the first and last UFO's I have ever seen. It was unbalancing and chilling. Everything for the rest of the night felt off-kilter. Like living in Dr Caligari's Cabinet.

Saturday March 28th

Last night's strange lights turned out to be Elon Musk's Space-X programme launching a multitude of satellites. I'm really bloody disappointed if I'm honest.

We received a letter from the Government today telling us that things will "get worse before they get better" and that "tighter restrictions could be implemented if necessary". But apparently the authors of this letter prevented the UK from joining the EU ventilator scheme because they "missed the email".

I am going to be furloughed as of April 1st because I cannot do my job. The furlough scheme ends in October. I'm not sure if the virus will be under control by then, but my boss is topping up my salary for the time being. Which is nice. I still have to work one day a week. This will be database housekeeping and gathering data for when we're all back again. Whenever that might be. And Johnson's got COVID-19.

Sunday March 29th

An NHS nurse died of COVID-19 today.

Monday March 31st

My Mum, along with other elderly and vulnerable people, have been advised to "Shield" themselves from today. This is basically House Arrest. My mother has enough food supplies put aside to last for a Nuclear Winter, so I think she'll be okay. I think she'll enjoy the challenge.

APRIL 2020

Wednesday April 1st (April Fool's Day)

First day of furlough today. The word 'furlough' derives from the Middle Low German 'verlōf', which means 'day boozing'. Pretty accurate as far as today goes, in that I've been sitting under the parasol in the back garden drinking gin and tonic and listening to Brainiac, Fiona Apple and Frank Sinatra all afternoon. And Baby Shark, as requested by the little kids next door. The uncanny weirdness we're living in is causing me to come suddenly awake during the darks of the night.

In the era of Samuel Pepys, it was accepted practice to have a 'First Sleep' and a 'Second Sleep'. People would arise from their beds after the first sleep to conduct their business in the early hours, carrying out all nature of activities and amusements, before returning to bed for the second.

Trump Comedy Gold Latest. It's Barack Obama's fault that there weren't any tests or information in 2016 about a virus that was only identified in 2019. I'm painting a fence panel, getting drunk and listening to disco music tomorrow. Seems the sensible thing to do under the circumstances.

Thursday April 2nd

Matt Hancock popped up suddenly today, looking like a reflection in the back of a tablespoon, to front the new daily Government briefing. Where in the name of fuck do these people come from? I've never met anyone even remotely like them in over fifty years of life. It's almost like they're from a different world. Or something.

Clap for Carers tonight. Someone up the road had an air horn and Linden had his trumpet. It was like two elephants having a barney.

And the windowsill tomatoes are growing!

Friday April 3rd

The Government have announced the construction of 'Nightingale Hospitals' for the expected forthcoming tsunami of COVID-19 victims. This is probably a good idea because the dam is bursting. Hotels are going to shelter homeless people during the crisis. This begs the question; considering the vast number of empty homes in Britain, why not keep that process going?

And RIP Bill Withers. You were the basis of my favourite ever joke.

Q: How do you turn a duck into a soul singer?
A: Put it in a microwave until its bill withers.

Saturday April 4th

Ah Christ. A five-year-old kid has died of COVID-19. We are now even more determined not to allow anyone near us and not to go anywhere unnecessary. Everything feels like it's falling apart. Nobody really knows what we're dealing with yet. Trump is squawking about something called hydroxychloroquine as being efficacious for COVID-19. I looked this stuff up. It's an anti-malarial pill which is also used in the treatment of lupus, and arthritis. The side effects sound appalling. Nobody knows how it works. Trump certainly doesn't know how it works. Trump doesn't know how a pencil works.

Far from being 'sorted' for PPE as announced by Johnson a couple of weeks ago, the British Medical Association today reported that there is an acute lack of it.

Sunday April 5th (Palm Sunday)

The Queen was on the telly tonight! She was like a big Mum. It was weird but nice. And Handshake Johnson's in hospital with Covid.

Monday April 6th

A 99-year-old WWII Army veteran, Captain Tom Moore, has started doing laps of his garden on a walking frame to raise funds for NHS Charities. He was on the telly and seems a twinkly chap. He has an accent like my Dad. My issue is this. Why does the NHS need support from charities or retired soldiers? I thought we had all paid for this via our taxes and National Insurance since

1948? I suppose our hard-earned tax money has gone on more important things. Like pointless, oil-and-money-driven wars. And career politicians' salaries and expenses.

Tuesday April 7th

Johnson's in intensive care with COVID-19.

Wednesday April 8th

Linzi took this today. Has there ever been a more bewildered-looking image?

Thursday April 9th

I took my melodica out for tonight's Clap for Carers and played some free-form jazz. It was a horrible noise, but it was loud. It sounded like a riot was going on in town!

Friday April 10th (Good Friday)

6,000 UK deaths now. If this doesn't make people finally sit up, take notice and behave, I don't have a clue what will. All they need to do is stay away from other people and wash the crap off their hands. From our hideous experience in Tesco today, the message still isn't getting through. Hancock popped up on our TV again today to announce that a "Herculean Effort" is being made to provide PPE to the NHS. According to friends of mine within the NHS, they haven't got any PPE whatsoever. Perhaps he meant Promethean?

First sleep concluded at two of the clock. Picked huge louse from crotch of breeches. Summoned Tarquin for scrollop, cheese and ale, which repast I enjoyed in the outhouse. After attending His Majesty, composed letters to Mr Bland and Lord Nolly concerning hats. Turgid performance of As You Like It at The Royal Court. By horse to Croydon to distribute my pamphlet regarding turbot, then carousing at the Blind Ewe where drunken Rafe Tollington was wont to display his rump until he was hanged to death from the balustrade. And so to bed.

Saturday April 11th

Trump's America has reached a COVID-19 death toll of 20,000. I can hardly believe this. There is a wilful and erratic toddler in charge of this vast nation and he's wilfully killing people because he's too busy playing golf.

I remembered today that when I was fifteen I went to a wedding reception with my girlfriend and got off with the bride.

Sunday April 12th (Easter Sunday)

The Government are "airbrushing out" hundreds of elderly people who have died at care homes from the COVID-19 death figures, according to the Care Sector.

10,000 people dead here., but Johnson's out of hospital so that's okay. He says he's "bursting with antibodies". He could prove this by actually bursting. I'd watch it!

We had chocolate. Too much chocolate. We too are bursting.

Tuesday April 14th

The UK death toll overtook China's yesterday.

Equally unbelievably, Trump announced he is going to withhold funding to the World Health Organisation. At this point I think we can safely say that we are now down the rabbit hole.

Thursday April 16th (Last Day of Passover)

I had my Testosterone injection today. Getting into the surgery was like a military exercise. The surgery itself is ostensibly shut. So, fully masked, I rang the bell. Nurse Helen answered, threw sanitiser at me, and gave me a fresh NHS-Issue Mask. From then on everything was normal, apart from the masks and gowns. Apparently (although not surprisingly) the nurses, doctors, and other surgery staff are being subjected to almost hourly abuse from people who go through life thinking it's all about them. Nurse Helen said they'd run out of goodies at the practice, so I picked up a couple of boxes of Heroes at lunch and dropped them off at the surgery.

Captain Tom Moore has completed his final lap. At the same time, Trump's America has reached an incredible 30,000 deaths, and he doesn't give a toss. Historically speaking, psychopathic leaders have always displayed utter contempt for the people who granted them their power.

Friday April 17th

My one-day-at-work a week is weird. All I can do is fanny about on the system and set things up for whenever this situation ends. My work is alien, because I'm used to talking to about forty people a day. But it's good news furlough-wise, because at least we still have some money coming in. Others aren't so fortunate.

Over in Trumpington-on-Bigot, he tweets "LIBERATE MINNESOTA!" and "LIBERATE MICHIGAN!" and then "LIBERATE VIRGINIA and save your great 2nd Amendment. It is under siege!" And into the streets they swarmed. Thousands of them, with about fifteen teeth between them. The rest of the planet, surely, must be shaking its head in disbelief and despair. We are. It's like living in the Horror Channel.

We ordered some raised beds today. With the way things are going we might need a level of Good Life self-sufficiency. Next stop - salmon farming.

Sunday April 19th

The semi-inflated Lord Fauntleroy that is Robert Jenrick MP says that the virus is having a "disproportionate impact" on BAME people. What a shocker. After years of austerity and the destruction of BAME communities by his filthy philosophy.

And, having now missed *four* chances to join the EU PPE acquisition scheme, Hancock says that he wishes he could wave a magic wand and have PPE fall onto him from the sky. I wish I had a magic wand too. It wouldn't be PPE. Perhaps a grand piano.

Meanwhile, Trump has stated that his loyal anti-social-distancing protestors were all following social-distancing rules. We saw the footage. You wouldn't have got a fag paper between them. And we didn't see one face covering.

Tuesday April 21st

I was up at 6am in readiness for our raised beds delivery. They arrived at seven and are about half the size I was expecting. They smell nice though.

I hate being right about this, but following the Cheltenham Festival, deaths in that area are now double the national average. But hey, someone made a fortune. I wager, however, that they weren't anywhere near fucking Cheltenham in April. A further 823 fatalities have been reported in the UK, which takes the total to 17,337.

According to Trump, it's now the Black Lives Matter protestors to blame for America's massive spike in cases. How convenient. However, we saw this footage as well, and most of the people taking part were masked.

Wednesday April 22nd

A friend tasked me to construct and demonstrate a face mask today. Half a roll of Sellotape and one bin bag later, I accepted the challenge. I only wish I'd have put a party squeaker in the mouthpiece.

Thursday April 23rd (Ramadan Starts)

Busy old day today. Mowing. Fence painting. Positioning the three raised beds without the use of sharp sand because I can't get hold of any. Planting peas, broad beans, runner beans and the tomato seedlings from the windowsill. Beautifying the raised bed area with leftover

Cloud Stones because it looked horrible. Taking the dog for a lengthy gambol. Making Sunday Dinner. Not to mention all the drinking I had to do.

Friday April 24th

At his daily briefing, or whatever it was, yesterday, Trump mooted the idea of injecting disinfectant to kill the coronavirus: He said, on record, "Is there a way we can do something like that, by injection inside or almost a cleaning?" You know that rabbit hole? We're through the other side and the world has gone mad. I'm going to spend more time in the garden.

In kinder and more sane news, a version of You'll Never Walk Alone recorded by Captain Tom Moore and Michael Ball to raise money for the NHS Charities Together fund has been released. Tom isn't exactly a vocalist but, right now, who cares?

Saturday April 25th

I saw some footage today of nurses being harassed by Trump supporters in the US. Violently harassed. Nurses. Observe, if you will, the empathy and intelligence of these brave people in the godforsaken intellectual backwater that is Donald Trump's America in 2020.

Piers Corbyn (Jeremy's brother) rocked up in Glastonbury today. This man, who I had never heard of, stood in the middle of our little town with a megaphone, shrieking "There is no pandemic!!" to a braying and hideous crowd of the selfish and entitled, none of whom were from Glastonbury. Piers Corbyn lives in London, so why he felt the need to travel to our town, in the least-affected region of the country, to bellow his ridiculous disinformation through a megaphone surrounded by smug foil-hatted dunces from who knows where, god knows. Thank you, Piers, and your sneering and well-heeled acolytes. We really want your disgusting pathogens. Another Anti-Lockdown gathering is planned for May 3rd apparently.

Trump backpedalled yesterday, saying that he was "asking a question sarcastically" about injecting disinfectant. He doesn't even know what sarcasm is. In the wake of his blithering idiocy, the manufacturers of the most popular disinfectant in America had to release the following statement: "Under no circumstance should our disinfectant products be administered into the human body". I also read that Trump's USA is not participating in an $8 billion WHO international effort to speed coronavirus testing and vaccine development. He's just like Jesus isn't he.

Monday April 27th

Sleep easy Britain. Johnson is back in Downing Street and is 'in charge' of the Government's response to the outbreak again.

Tuesday April 28th

Matt Hancock said today that Care Home death numbers will now be included in the daily death toll. It seems that they haven't been included thus far. Who'd have thunk it? Meanwhile, in The Trump Asylum, the tragic death toll has topped 50,000.

Wednesday April 29th

From 4,419 deaths, the COVID-19 mortality rate has magically rocketed to 26,097 when Care Homes deaths are included. The bastards! This country is run by liars and murderers. These people have been lying to us for decades, so why on earth should we believe them when they tell us that it's safe to go back to work and start paying our lovely, lovely taxes again?

And talking about knackers, mine are having a rough time of it today. While I was getting out of bed I somehow managed to kick myself in the bollocks. And I've just crossed my legs and nearly popped one.

Thursday April 30th

Today the Government stated that the UK is past the peak of the COVID-19 outbreak, but that that the country "must not risk a second spike". They announced that there will be a comprehensive plan for easing the first lockdown next week. Having been to both Tesco and Aldi this week I predict another, huge, almost unstoppable wave within weeks. Why? Because people are stupid, and the government only cares about money and the people who have it. Apart from less traffic on the roads because office-based people are working from home, I have seen very little evidence that there has ever been an actual 'lockdown' since early April.

Captain Tom Moore celebrated his 100th birthday today He's been promoted to Honorary Colonel by the Queen and he raised £32 Million for the NHS. But, if we're honest, he shouldn't have had to. Not really.

MAY 2020

Friday May 1st (Beltane)

Happy Beltane! For once we didn't go up the Tor for carousing and watching the sun rise like we usually do. We usually see the sunrise with some friends, then pop over to Street for a Full English. Then, once afternoon comes, we meet back up with our friends in the pub and get uproariously drunk.

Instead, it was another busy old furlough day. I popped up another bird house and cut some branches off the massive tree that have been blocking the sun from the raised beds. With cider. We'll have a Beltane Fire later if I'm still conscious.

Saturday May 2nd

Today was World Naked Gardening Day. As ever I am happy to participate.

Monday May 4th

News at Ten Headline... When will the Premier League start again? Seriously?? In the actual, real world, people are dying horribly. Football?? Anyone who has this at the front of their minds needs to have a serious grown-up word with themselves. Although Love Island has been cancelled. Every cloud.

First sleep concluded at 3.30 of the clock. Mended large moth hole in pantaloon crutch. Summoned Patsy for pilchards, pork, plum posset and port, which repast I enjoyed in the parlour. After attending His Majesty, penned two letters to Sir Robin and Mr Twombly regarding loam. Triumphant performance of Dryden's The Wild Gallant at The Royal Court. Then by litter to Garlic Row for distribution of my pamphlet "One Man, One Arse". Carousing at The Padfoot Arms where poor Lord Stuntney was eaten by a bear. And so to bed.

Wednesday May 6th

On this fine day, Johnson announced that the UK would start to lift COVID-19 lockdown restrictions next week, following the news that the UK death toll became the highest in Europe yesterday. He also "bitterly regrets" the COVID-19 crisis in care homes. I think the phrase is 'Jesus Wept'.

I've started painting the fence because there's not much else to do for six days of the week. I bought a huge vat of Ronseal Fencelife and, because I have more actual time than I can ever remember, have decided to do it properly by hand with a brush. Stuart next door said he's thinking of doing his as well, so, I poured some of the paint into a container for him. It's actually very nice, having a beer or a cider in the garden and chatting with the neighbours in the sun, and fence painting.

Thursday May 7th

It was my Mum's 85th birthday today. With it being VE Day tomorrow I called her and played The Coldstream Guards thumping out Happy Birthday down the phone. We bought her two novels from a series she's reading about Henry VIII's wives. She said, "Ooooh thank you! The doorbell rang this morning, and my patio was full of gifts from the neighbours! Flowers. A really lovely clematis in a pot. Boxes of chocolates. Liver." She was particularly happy about the liver.

Somebody called The Baroness Harding of Winscombe has been appointed Head of NHS Test and Trace. I've never heard of her, so I looked her up. She breeds racehorses and is married to the Tory MP for Weston-Super-Mare. No surprise there. She was also Marketing Director for Thomas Cook, was very high in the chain-of-command at Woolworths, Tesco and Sainsbury's, and was the first CEO of Talk Talk. She has cocked up everything she's ever clapped eyes on, and one NHS spokesman said, on learning of her new appointment, that "she seems to be failing upwards". It's nice to know that this vital service isn't being run by doctors or a tech company or anyone else who knows what the bloody hell they're doing.

It eventually took 50% of a Zopiclone tablet to silence my shrieking mind last night. Possibly not that wise on top of Pimm's and gin, but there we are. I got over nine hours sleep and apparently there was some vivid dreaming. We had a chat about it today and concluded that it's a combination of 'lockdown', ADHD, the general outlandishness of life and the full supermoon we've just had. The moon has always had an impact on my ability to sleep.

Friday May 8th (VE Day)

VE Day Bank Holiday Weekend has started well. I had more Pimm's, and Stuart next door brought us round a tasty cauliflower cheese that he'd made. I listened to Glenn Miller all afternoon while I was painting and gardening.

Just before I turned in tonight, I let Jack into the back garden. He usually goes out for a quick wee and wanders back in. This isn't our nightly promenade around the front and cuddle on the path, just a brief piddle before bed. I hissed for him to come in, but he didn't. I took the torch out and he was standing on the lawn looking scared. His way back to the house was being blocked by three great big hedgehogs who were just sitting there looking at him.

Saturday May 9th

I reached the most problematic part of the fence painting today. We have a huge Californian Lilac to the right of the garden, which butts up against the fence itself. I had to get the brush both under and right through the sharp spiky limbs. This involved getting badly scratched, covered in tiny blue petals and grumped at by bees. Once I'd managed it, I came into the house with my hair full of twigs, and said to Linzi, "It's like a jungle out there… it makes me wonder how I keep from going under!" She ignored me so I went back outside.

Sunday May 10th

Took dog out.
Came home.
Made a sandwich.
Spotted a blowfly.
Whacked it with the electric fly bat.
Electrocuted fly landed on my sandwich.
Made further sandwich.

Monday May 11th

Johnson has announced a plan for an end to the lockdown and says that people who cannot work from home should return to the workplace but avoid public transport. I expect to see inner-city bricklayers and sheet metal workers being ferried to and from their places of work by their chauffeurs.

Sometimes, when I am having difficulties getting to sleep, like now, it comforts me to imagine that I am back in the Late Jurassic and the very place I am laying is teeming with vast, huge-eyed, sinuous aquatic reptiles.

Tuesday May 12th

State schools are going to reopen in some form. Eerily, though, I cannot find any information about those *Other* schools reopening. You know. Eton. Rugby. Harrow. No news there at all.

We bought some Tesco Finest Cave-Aged Cheddar and Bramley Apple Sauce Crisps. They tasted and smelled like a marathon-runner had rinsed his feet in Essence of Disco Gusset.

The new Government slogan is "Stay Alert. Control The Virus. Save Lives." Alert? I tried being vigilant once and Linzi said I just looked dodgy.

Wednesday May 13th

My suspicion is that when the devastating, predictable and preventable second wave occurs, the Government will be able to shirk responsibility by saying that we weren't 'alert' enough. And what the hell is all this Bill Gates stuff?
On the subject of fantasists, if we're "beating the virus" and "the curve has flattened", why has the furlough scheme been extended for another five months?

Thursday May 14th

I took my guitar onto the front lawn for Clap for Carers tonight and played and sang It's All About You by McFly. They're great musicians. I'm not. But it was nice. We saw our first swallows and swifts tonight. And I realised that I can't hear the word "buffoon" without picturing somebody inflating a toad.

Jack has a tick on his groin. We can't get anywhere near it. Even carrots won't distract him. And I don't fancy getting my arm gnawed off by a Husky.

Friday May 15th

It occurs to me that this whole thing is class-based. COVID-19 isn't an indiscriminate Grim Reaper harvesting people willy-nilly. As it's pneumonic, it is obviously going to target those whose livelihoods or living conditions necessitate being in close proximity to others, rather than those who can conduct their work via Zoom or Skype. And it will most certainly be staying away from those fragrant people who call the Upper Middle Classes "bastards what have to go shooting on Sundays", because they don't have to lift a finger for their inherited booty. So, for an avid Hilary Mantel reader like myself, it's comforting to know that nothing has changed in this country since the Tudor period, when the wealthy would up-sticks out of cities in times of plague and sweating sickness and let the plebs die in their thousands.

Who Wants to Be A Millionaire started again tonight. I like this show because I occasionally know all the answers. What the hell has happened to Jeremy Clarkson's voice? "Let's play Who Wants to be A MillioNAAAOOOOARAOARGHAAAAIR!"

Saturday May 16th

There was a march in London today, demonstrating against COVID-19 restrictions and 'lockdown'. Much like the Piers Corbyn fiasco, the collective intellect of those attending can be summarised by this placard. And probably the bloke to the right of it. My right. And your right.

We caught Gavin Williamson, who is apparently the Education Secretary, doing a press conference. I believe the remotely based journalists had been told not to ask certain questions.

My one question would be this:

"Gavin, why are public schools like Eton, Harrow, Rugby and so on, and the Preparatory Schools, not opening their doors until September *at the earliest*? Are the children and staff at these schools particularly vulnerable, or could there possibly be another reason? Gavin? Gavin??"

Tonight was Eurovision Night. We always love this because it's hilarious and there are occasional precious gems like Conchita Wurst. Of course, the final has been cancelled, but Graham Norton delivered a wonderfully camp celebration of the whole thing. We probably enjoyed it even more than usual.

After a trip to Tesco for carrots, a call to the vets, a lengthy search online for information about parasites and a near mauling, we had a proper look at Jack's tick today, it turned out to be his willy.

Sunday May 17th

The Government has started running a 'Hey, Get Out There and Enjoy Yourselves, Britain!' television campaign. For us, the killer is a drone shot of Glastonbury Tor right at the end. It's Sunday today. Next Saturday the place will be heaving with people from all over the bloody country. I posted on Facebook: "I doubt that anyone I know is this thick. But, just in case, please stay away from the West Country next weekend. It's nothing personal, but we don't want you here. Nothing's open. Everyone will tell you and your viruses to leave. We are the least COVID-19-affected area of the country and we would like to keep it that way. So, with best wishes… Fuck Off."

Monday May 18th

I found out today that NHS nurses from overseas are still having to pay a surcharge for putting their lives on the line in Britain during a viral pandemic. The Tories should hang their heads in abject shame.

That TV campaign is really going for it. So we're bracing ourselves for an influx of dullards this weekend for a good old pathogenic jolly. I may write a music hall song about it. "Oh! Mister Darwin!" or something.

The Tories have suddenly become concerned about children from vulnerable backgrounds suddenly. Something to do with schools. They'll get over it.

In happier news, superspreader Piers Corbyn has been arrested.

Tuesday May 19th

I had to pick a prescription up from Tesco today and haven't felt as vulnerable since this began. Most people in there appear to believe that the pandemic is Over and that We're Back to Normal. I suppose this level of idiocy is just what the grandees at The Mail, Sun, Express and in the Government are hoping for.

There was an advert on the telly today for a heart-monitor called KardiaMobile. Apparently Mark Spitz has got aphids.

Wednesday May 20th (World Bee Day)

Took jack out.
Bar opened.
Cut some bits off the big tree that is blocking the sun from my raised beds.
Painted more of the fence.
Developed a taste for elderflower tonic water. It's both sweet and refreshing.

Johnson said today that the UK would have 'World-Beating' track and trace system by next month, with 25,000 contact tracers tracing 10,000 people a day. This will all be down to the Powerhouse of Achievement that is The Baroness 'Dido' Harding of Winscombe.

The Tourette's was bad today. Linzi has vowed to beat me about the head and neck if I don't stop saying "Perf with Surf".

Friday May 22nd

Hello Hello Hello! What's going on here then Mr Cummings? Huge coverage of him being questioned by police about a breach of his own lockdown rules. I've always wondered what his job interview for Chief Advisor to the Prime Minister was like.

"Please sit down, Mr Cummings."
"Thank you."
"So, what are your qualifications for advising the Government about the profound social and economic issues the country faces and possibly a novel and incurable disease?"
"Well, I came up with two misleading Brexit slogans and lied about NHS funding on the side of a bus."
"Jolly good. Here's your desk."

Saturday May 23rd

I have decided to make a mosaic to go on the front-facing bit of one of our garden steps. It will be of Glastonbury Tor in some form. I placed a wanted ad on the local Marketplace Facebook page for some tiles this morning. I also bought some pilchards from Tesco. The last time I had pilchards I sent the tin back to Glenryck in a plastic bag, complaining about all the little rubbery bits.

Glenryck sent back a pound note taped to a handwritten letter, saying "The rubbery bits are part of the pilchards". I didn't believe them because I had always liked pilchards as a child and there certainly weren't any rubbery bits. Today's pilchards went in the bin because there were rubbery bits. Something sinister has happened to the pilchard.

More news on the Cummings scandal! It appears that he breached the lockdown rules by taking a 264-mile trip to his parent's place in Durham. From the footage outside his house, it looks like his neighbours want to give him a right pasting.

Monday May 25th (Early May Bank Holiday)

Dominic Cummings held a news conference and Q&A session in the lovely Downing Street rose garden today. I broke off my mosaic work to come in and watch it. It was brilliant.

1. On March 27th, the day Johnson found out he had COVID-19, Cummings received a call from his wife to say she had been sick.

2. Cummings rushed home and, as the evening went on, her condition improved. So he returned to work.

3. Later that night, though, he started to think that his now symptomless wife had contracted COVID-19, and that he would probably catch it as well.

4. Fearing that they were both about to become too weak to care for their four-year-old son, they all drove the 264 miles to Durham, non-stop. They arrived at midnight and stayed at a house on Cummings' parents land, near to where his sister, who had promised to help with childcare, lived.

5. The next day, Cummings was convinced that he had COVID-19, so he didn't get up.

6. On March 30th the Government announced that Cummings had COVID-19 symptoms and was isolating at home, failing to mention that this 'home' was in Durham, contravening his own legislation.

7. Cummings' son was taken to hospital on April 2nd with what Cummings described as COVID-19 symptoms.

8. Cummings' son was collected, perfectly well, by Cummings the next day, April 3rd. Although he drove to and from the hospital, he said that he was too sick to get out of the car.

9. Over a week later, On April 12th, Cummings felt well enough to make the journey back to London. He was, however, concerned that COVID-19 had affected his vision. He loaded his wife and child into their car and drove 30 miles to the local beauty spot of Barnard Castle to make sure he could see properly.

10. The next day Cummings and his family returned to London.

Breaking Lockdown If I Did It

"Our monarch desires the most severe of deaths for this felony and therefore you shall, at Her Majesty's pleasure, be taken from your dwelling to a public place and there you shall be hung by the neck and removed from said rope while still you live. You shall then be cut from sternum to groin. Your vitals shall be pulled from your body and incinerated. Your manhood shall be severed and then likewise burned while you observe such. Your body then will be shackled to four fine horses who shall, upon Her Majesty's approval, tear thyself in four. Thereafter shall your parts be displayed from London to York."

As today was a Bank Holiday, residents of beauty spots throughout Britain were treated to vast plagues of tourists, none of whom seemed to have heard of social distancing, and some of whom thought it was fine to take a crap on beaches, in woods and on footpaths. Again, Great British Public, what a literal pile of shit you really are.

Tuesday May 26th

It occurred to me last night that I've tried to live an anarchistic life for decades, and now I get to do it for real. We are cannon fodder in a national Economics-based Petrie-Dish, including our primary-age children. So, again, we're making our own decisions. Fuck the Government.

Of all available lifeforms, it's Piers Morgan who is sticking it into the politicians! I'll only feel anything like normal when I can comfortably start hating him again.

Tonight, we saw the unbelievably horrific footage of a police officer in Minneapolis kneeling on a black man's neck yesterday, in broad daylight, with witnesses filming, until the black man died.

Wednesday May 27th

I had a response to my wanted ad for tiles and picked up three heavy, free boxes of swirly green bathroom ones from a woman down the road.

My friend Mandy dropped off some Steampunk gardening goggles for me today. The hay fever is terrible this year because the weather is so glorious. Along with a mask for my respiratory system they'll keep the pollen out of my eyes while I'm mowing things.

On the subject of masks, why are people just chucking them about all over the place? There are loads of the things in hedges and gutters all over town. They are hardly a bulky or sanitary item. People are disgusting. Especially, as reported today, the UK now has the highest COVID-19 death rate in the world. That's ***The World!!***

Thursday May 28th

The Government must be delighted that their television advertisements suggesting people 'Get Out And Spend Your Money (safely, but… y'know… just spend your money eh)' have worked a treat. We had to go out in the car today and spent most of our time doing a Tourist Slalom, as great herds of them wandered aimlessly across the roads in front of us. And now that people have carte blanche to leap in their cars and spread their bugs all over the country, we're avoiding the centre of town like the plague. Literally. Morrison's was full of them as well. Second Wave you say? I should say so!

Friday May 29th

Protests, many of them under the Black Lives Matter banner, are taking place all over the world following George Floyd's murder (for it was) at the hands of a Minneapolis policeman called Derek Chauvin last Monday. This police officer knelt on George Floyd's neck for several minutes until George Floyd was dead. In response to these demonstrations, the malevolent Trump tweeted that he would send in the National Guard. He then tweeted, "when the looting starts, the shooting starts." In a country where everyone is armed to the teeth, which saw the early deaths of Martin Luther King Jr, JFK, John Lennon and countless schoolchildren, how is this demon still drawing breath?

Saturday May 30th

I'm having problems getting my mosaic started, mainly because I have never worked with tiles before, but also because the free green ones I got are quarter of an inch thick and as hard as iron. I'm going to use those ones to go on the front of the other steps and get some sample ones from Topps Tiles and some proper mosaic pieces from the internet for the mosaic itself.

Sunday May 31st

It has been so hot already this year that the ground has shrunk and the front lawn has pulled away where it meets the footpath. This afternoon I made a pourable soil-and-water 'slurry' to fill the gap. Four bucketfuls later and, although it has amply stuffed the void, it looks like someone has had a dreadful faecal accident in the front garden.

JUNE 2020

Monday June 1ˢᵗ (Whit Monday)

Kinzi told me today that being with me is like living with a Bird of Paradise, which I was really chuffed about. Then she explained that it's because I'm constantly and pointlessly showing off and poncing about all over the house.

I ordered a Black Lives Matter tee shirt today. In the toxic and bigoted Post-Brexit world we're living in via Trump, Johnson and the rest, the more white people who stand up for what is right, the better life will be, eventually, for everyone. That's what I believe anyway.

Tuesday June 2ⁿᵈ

We're starting to hear about something called the R Rate. R is the average number of people that one infected person will pass on a virus to. For instance, measles has an R Rate of 15 in populations without immunity. This means, on average, that one infected person will spread measles to 15 others within that population. News reports about COVID-19 are beginning to refer to the R Rate as a measurement of how the virus is, or isn't, spreading. "R" stands for "Reproduction". The R Rate in Somerset has doubled over the last couple of weeks. What does this tell me? It tells me that Johnson and Dido's "World Beating" Test and Trace system isn't working in any way. It tells me that the Money First philosophy of the Tories is manslaughter at best and murder at worst. It tells me that those hordes of tourists brought more to the West Country than their fat old wallets. And it tells me to look to the filthy leftie Socialist country of New Zealand, who haven't had a case of COVID-19 for weeks.

Saturday June 5th

I woke up this morning with a severe case of *Incertocalvitum Pugil*, which is being unsure whether Henry Cooper is still alive or not. Something deep in my heart misses the homoerotic glory-days of Henry, Kevin Keegan and The Great Smell of Brut.

Walking back with Jack just now there was a lot of screaming, hollering and general carrying on around the corner. From what we could hear, a couple of male neighbours are going to "kill each other", and they're both going to be "dead". We have Pimm's and folding chairs, so watching the finale of Chernobyl may have to wait. It's quite cold tonight, but one of them has already got his top off. Classic! Although in this case I suspect it's because all of his tops are minging and in the wash. Or maybe on the floor. I'm not judging. Yes I am. We both have Strictly-style paddles at the ready to give our scores at the end.

Sunday June 6th

Sadly, the Fight of The Century petered out last night. There was the occasional Jeremy-Clarkson-like "Whoooooargh!" but that was about it. Two Zeros from us.

It has just been announced that all NHS workers will have to wear PPE from June 15th. Twelve weeks ago the Government knew all about this pandemic, but took no action whatsoever. Johnson said that PPE was 'sorted' I remember. And because of his arrogant incompetence, NHS workers now have to change their face masks every twenty minutes because they are completely unfit for purpose.

We had some Mr Kipling After Dinner Mint Fancies after tea. They taste like Aquafresh.

Monday June 7th

There was a huge Black Lives Matter demonstration in Bristol today. The denouement was the tearing down of much-lauded local slaver Edward Colston's statue in central Bristol, rolling it through the streets, and dumping it into the harbour.
Possibly because of this, I had my first conversation about White Privilege today. Although I have been active, through music and otherwise, in anti-racist activities since the 1970's, this is a concept that had never crossed my mind. It was a real lesson. Dee, our Zimbabwean neighbour, came across the road for a socially distant chat about her dog. Over the last few years, I have written

letters for her, her kids and her partner to various Government departments and schools, because of issues the family were having. But actual White Privilege had never been a topic. As soon as I brought it up, Dee said "Yeah. Absolutely!" Then, as we talked, it became clear that, regardless of the very real struggles I have had throughout my life, my skin colour has never been an issue. And it made me realise how much harder things would have been without my White Privilege. I have been educated today. And not before time.

I have finally admitted to myself that I can't see properly and made an appointment at SpecSavers. And when I was going to the bathroom tonight, I sang to Linzi: "Oh! I'm on the train to Tiddle Town. Next Stop, Pooh Corner!"

Tuesday June 8th

Tonight I sat in the garden on my own, listening to Bach and weeping silently about the hateful world in which we live.

Wednesday June 9th

A friend posted the following on Social Media today:

So, first real proper post in a while but it's fully needed. Listen to black people if they say your words are damaging. Understand that, as a white person, you will not understand the oppression that black people endure (therefore reverse racism isn't a thing, you are NOT oppressed). You have not experienced oppression due to your skin colour if you are white. Your problems are not because of your skin colour. You benefit from the system due to your skin colour. Generational wealth is a thing. I understand that I am mixed-race and therefore I have certain privileges, but I am obviously black, and I identify as black. White people will not understand the struggles as they have not faced them. But they can try.

I went to SpecSavers. It was very professional. Hand sanitiser. Only me in the shop. Visor-wearing optician. I wonder whether they'd have treated me so kindly if they knew that I was taking their twenty-quid prescription and buying some cheapo online specs with it?

Thursday June 10th

Measuring pupillary distance for the purpose of ordering glasses only is more of a mission that we thought. We downloaded and printed out a 'measuring template' but the results were different every time. In the end we just sent off the average distance. Linzi says it's because my eyes keep swivelling about. I ordered two pairs (one general and one reading) from an online store for less than a glasses case would have been from SpecSavers.

The Government announced that households will shortly be able to meet in what it's calling Support Bubbles. The only bubbles we're having are the ones in beer, cider and Aeros. And Trump is going to start having rallies again soon. Good. His evangelical followers are all 'Washed in the Blood of Jesus' anyway, so they have nothing to fear.

Friday June 11th

It was such a lovely day that I played the largo part of Holst's "Jupiter, The Bringer of Jollity" loudly on my Bluetooth speaker and got Linzi to film me galloping about in the garden wearing my new t shirt.

Saturday June 13th (Sudden Exaltation of Statues Day)

And so it was written, that all across the land, proud Englishmen gathered to protect the precious statues of the great and the good from the days of Glorious Empire. Chests puffed with pride, they guarded their great effigies against harm by urinating all over them, drinking vats of beer, attacking the police and singing the National Anthem. Although, it should be noted, they did not know the words after the first verse.

On being asked why he and his fellows felt the need to gather and defend his local monument, one gallant said, "Well it's our history ain't it. English history. British history. It's important that we know our country's history. It's nuffin to do with being a racialist."

A time-traveller might ask this gilded patriot his opinion of his cherished statue way back in March.

Time-Travelling Interviewer: So, what are your thoughts about statuary?

Gilded Patriot: You looking for a fucking kicking?

First sleep concluded at two thirty of the clock. Brief yet melodic rehearsal on the fardle-dardle in the withdrawing room in preparation for our Friday recital. Summoned Rollo for blood sausage, gurnard and Malmsey, which repast I enjoyed in the scullery. After attending His Majesty, took a bracing swim in The Serpentine then buried a great wheel of Parmesan in the garden. Rousing performance of Etherege's The Man of Mode at the Royal Court, then a visit to Regents Park Zoological Garden to see new tapeworm exhibit.

Carousing in The Drowning Pig, where Barrington was fatally stabbed in the throat. And so to bed.

Sunday June 14th

I'm getting Fuck Off Fatigue. Every time the news comes on, I think (or yell) "Fuck OFF!" Racists. Politicians. Republicans. Tories. COVID-19-Deniers are a new target for this ire.

Monday June 15th

If a tree falls in the forest and Linzi doesn't hear it, is it still my fault?

Tuesday June 16th

Non-essential shops reopened yesterday. The retailers have installed Perspex screens and floor markings to keep people two metres apart. While the scenes from the beaches and public areas over the Bank Holidays and weekends weren't repeated, in that people weren't taking a dump in the aisles, the massive queues at Nike and Primark were astonishing.

New Zealand announced its first COVID-19 case in nearly a month. And it came in from the UK.

Friday June 19th

Hancock announced yesterday that the Track and Trace system is changing. *From* what *to* what? I've yet to hear of anyone being either Tracked or Traced. The people employed to do this are having to watch Netflix all day because nothing that The Baroness "Dido" Harding of Winscombe has put in place works. I think her nickname could be a typo.

Thrice I have been to a supermarket this week and, on each occasion, have had to give at least one fellow shopper a steely glare and ask them to respect my personal space. They're simply oblivious.

Me: Surely people aren't really this stupid? Considering there are so many new cases of COVID-19 every single day? All the deaths? The terrible news footage? They can't seriously think it's all over?

The Universe: You better believe it, Matey!!

We've just seen a Senokot ad on the telly and agree that, although neither of us have ever taken laxatives, we certainly wouldn't do so just before going to bed.

Sunday June 21st (Father's Day)

Jack and I are celebrating Father's Day by blaming each other for the variety of repulsive smells in this room.

Tuesday June 23rd

Never one to err on the side of caution when cash is involved, Johnson announced today that the UK's 'national hibernation' is coming to an end. He said that the Government are relaxing all COVID-19 restrictions including the two metre social distancing rule. In my experience, for the bulk of the British populace, this will have little impact, as they've just been sauntering through their lives with no regard for anyone else anyway. I'm gladdened that we're possibly coming out of this, but I fear that Johnson's announcement will be construed as 'Let's party cos we won WWII'. There's a lot of Rule Britannia going around at the moment and that attitude isn't going to stop a fatal virus. Distancing and respect just might.

We purchased some facemasks today. Sod what the Government says about it. Asia has far more experience of these viruses and they wear them as a matter of course. Mine is an Anarchy one!

I had my testosterone injection this evening. After the understandably rigid COVID-19 procedure to get in, during the procedure, Nurse Helen said that the needle was "too short" for some reason and that she had to sort of gouge it about a bit. I passed out cold on the couch in her room for five minutes. And having written this I am about to do so again.

Wednesday June 24th

Because I have to take a whole bunch of tablets after I eat in the evening (for gout, for restless legs and for being mental) Linzi ordered me a pill-organiser or 'dossette box' last month, so I could keep up to date with re-ordering my prescriptions and so that I wouldn't keep forgetting to take them. Both of these circumstances are traditional for people with ADHD. Here is this month's pill-organiser as it looked today. I'm chucking it out.

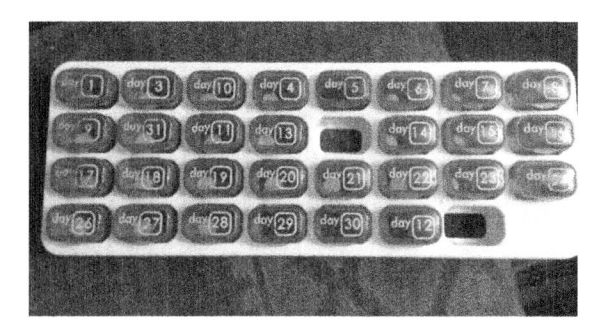

Thursday June 25th

33 tons of crap were left on the beaches of Bournemouth today, including plenty of actual crap. Thousands of Liverpool fans have descended on Anfield to celebrate their team's victory in the Premier League. And there was a big street party held in Brixon tonight.

Friday June 26th

This Month In Policing

Bournemouth: Mainly white people. Thousands on beach. Major incident announced. Day drinking. Fights. Three stabbings. Anti-Social Behaviour. Public defecation. No social distancing. Police use a light-handed approach, which is largely ineffective.

Liverpool: Mainly white people. Thousands inundate Anfield in celebration of a Championship win. No social distancing. No police in evidence whatsoever. The BBC report these events as: "Emotional Liverpool supporters tell of their delight at first English title win…"

Brixton: Mainly black people. Street party. No social distancing. Huge numbers of police immediately deployed on grounds of 'no social distancing'. Tensions escalate. Territorial Support Group (formerly SPG), who are reserved for severe public disorder situations, are sent in. Many injuries and arrests.

Saturday June 27th

It was so hot today that I wore my kilt. You have no idea how comfortable a kilt can be on a hot and sultry day. As a Western male I don't often experience the simple delight of having vortices of air-conditioning coursing around my unmentionables. The only issue is that when I waft coolly past the coffee table, I keep knocking things off it with the sort of enlarged 'bustle' bit that pokes out at the back. The final victim was Linzi's glass of cider. So I'm now in my undercrackers. Let's see if my arse alone is enough to send things crashing to the floor.

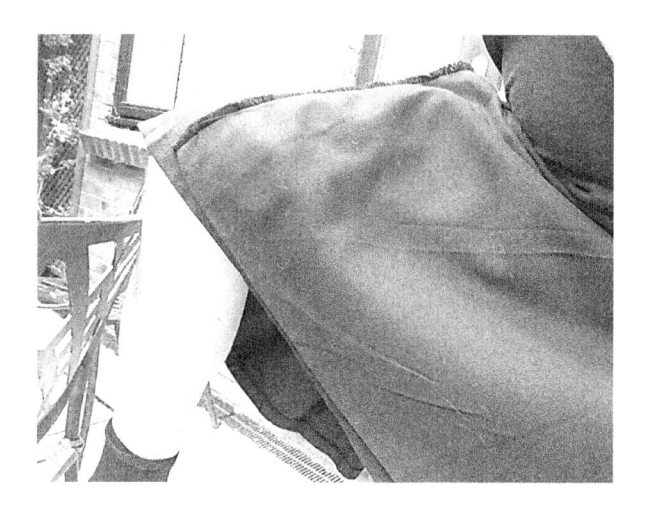

Sunday June 28th

Priti Patel popped up today to smirk that the UK's first local lockdown is likely be applied in Leicester and parts of Leicestershire due to the very high virus rates there. This does nothing, really, but prove that these half-baked National 'lockdowns' have had no impact. Scientists also warned that the country is "on a knife-edge" regarding next month's easing of this lockdown. As UK deaths from COVID-19 now stand at a staggering 43,550, I suppose Tory COVID-19 policies translate to He Who Dies the Richest Wins.

Now that I have some tools, the mosaic work is coming along nicely. Tiles are, once you get used to their nature, much like stones to manipulate, in as much as they are brittle and bloody awkward. This is where I am right now, as far as the design goes. It is supposed to represent Glastonbury Tor. The left-hand side is 'at night' with indigo and dark green hues, and the right is 'daytime', all sunny with bright blues. And I have managed to carve a heart for the centre of the sun out of a bright red tile and the sun's rays and the moon and a star.

Tuesday June 30th

I only realised today that when Lizzo sings about her DM's, she doesn't mean her Doc Martens.

JULY 2020

Wednesday July 1st

Linzi's a bit poorly. It's not COVID-19. She has a bit of a cold.

At a bizarre press-conference today, Trump stated the following when asked about COVID-19: "I think we're going to be very good with the coronavirus. I think that, at some point, that's going to sort of disappear, I hope." Relax, America.

Face coverings (masks) are possibly going to be mandatory soon, after months of Johnson and the Tories harumphing about it being un-British. My Anarchy mask is so well made that I have a job breathing with it on. I may repurpose it as a posing pouch, especially in this heat. We've got quite a selection of masks now, and we've been sporting them in shops since early June. I think we look cute.

Thursday July 2nd

With the USA's daily COVID-19 cases doubling to about 50,000, a higher number than they had right at the start the pandemic, Trump said today that the pandemic is "getting under control".

Linzi's illness has reminded me that trying to be silent in a quiet room is impossible. Going to bed last night and getting up this morning looked and sounded like a Norman Wisdom film had rogered a firework display.

Friday July 3rd

Great Britain is Back in Business! The easing of lockdown on Saturday is "our biggest step yet on the road to recovery" according to Johnson. Remember that this is the man whose master at Eton commented "he thinks the rules don't apply to him". The man about whom Charles Moore, who was his editor at The Daily Telegraph, claimed in an interview with The Times that he would just "wing it", saying, "He was always late for all his columns. It was a nightmare." The man who, after his unilateral decision to suspend parliament, which was ruled unlawful by the Supreme Court, Jeremy Corbyn said: "He thought he could do whatever he liked just as he always does. He thinks he's above us all." And the man about whom his own father said, "He just wants to be King of The World." So, do we take any notice of anything he says? Ever? This is legitimised murder. These are people's lives. This is a cull. As a case in point, 30,000 more care home residents in England and Wales have died this year than last. I don't know for sure, but I'm taking a wild stab-in-the-dark that neither Johnson nor his Tory pals have had to rely on Care Homes at any point in their families' history.

Saturday July 4th (Cloud's Birthday)

Trump: "99% of COVID-19 cases are totally harmless". I hope that the Evangelical God his supporters keep hollering about is listening. They're going to need him.

I just called Linzi a pedant. She said, "What do you mean by pedant?" I replied "Twat." She said, quite rightly, "That's not what pedant means."

Leicester and the surrounding area is now in that Local Lockdown. Divided country anyone? BAME people treated differently anyone?

Sunday July 5th

Last night the pubs opened again. We welcome this, but it still seems to be coated with Little Ingerland The Queen Mum, Gawd Bless 'Er. And for the life of me I still don't understand: "If you can't work from home, you must go to work." Why? If the furlough scheme is supporting people like me then why not all the men and women in factories and building sites and so on? We need things like food and nappies and toilet roll and pharmaceuticals and, sadly, coffins. But, once again, it can't be beyond this government's imagination to isolate the people who work in these sectors and, for a very short time, track, trace and isolate this part of the workforce? The virus would then have nowhere to go. I'm sick of hearing myself say this every day. I could weep.

First sleep concluded at four of the clock. Admonished passing constable for making water against Gelert's memorial, then summoned Tansy for lamprey, poke and owl, which repast I enjoyed in the great pantry. After attending His Majesty, penned two letters to Master Dobbin and Lord Christopher regarding scurf. Starchy performance of Dryden's "The Death of Minty" at The Royal Court. Then by sedan chair to Rotten Row for the double hanging. Carousing at The Stinking Eel, where Sir M was wont to display his sweetbreads on a trowel until Tobias Quigg flattened them with a whaling iron. And so to bed.

Monday July 6th

The lunatic UK Government has decided that overseas holidays are a good idea again. Meanwhile, we have our car rigged with anti-Great British Public products. Hand sanitiser. Antibacterial wipes. And our usual facemasks. We have also started running sterilising wipes over all our shopping and incoming mail. This isn't just borne from COVID-19. I have been disgusted by the way most people assume that everyone wants their filthy infections for years. The pandemic has just made my behaviour appear vaguely normal.

The COVID-19 death toll in the USA has now reached 140,000.

Wednesday July 8th

In 1952 my singing great-uncle, Wally Billycock King, who did turns at Working Men's Clubs along with his wife all around the Midlands with picks and shovels strung up like guitars and banjos, lent Engelbert Humperdinck £5.00.

Engelbert Humperdinck never paid him back. The cheap, orange, gravy-voiced, name-pilfering, Eurovision-losing, gorilla-chested, hamster-faced thieving old twat.

Thursday July 9th

Bruce Dart, Director of the Tulsa County Health Department in the USA said today: "The past two days we've had almost five-hundred COVID-19 cases… and we know we had several large events (Trump Rally) a little over two weeks ago, which is about right. So I guess we just connect the dots."

This man, the President of the United States of America, is going out of his way to kill his own people. Proof positive that he is a psychopath. That ability to distance himself from others' pain and hurt? It makes me wonder about the future of our species. We can be a godforsaken and cruel animal.

Secretary of State for Digital, Culture, Media and Sport, Oliver Dowden, swam to the surface like a Sealife Exhibit today to announce that UK gyms will reopen from 25 July. At every turn during this crisis, the Government is patently asking itself what Canute would have done. Handy partial anagram as well.

Linzi just came outside and shoved 'a Scooby Snack' into my chops. I guess we'll be back in the Mystery Machine earlier than I was anticipating.

Friday July 10th

I have mastered the art of tile cutting. Armed with this new skill, I sliced some of the big, thick green ones to go on the steps below and above the mosaic's destination. Then I rushed to Proper Job and bought some cheap tile adhesive and stuck the first steps-worth on. I just need to leave them to dry.

The UK's official COVID-19 death toll has increased by 148. This means at least 44,798 people have died with Covid-19 in the UK, as of today.

Sunday July 12th

I embarked on the grouting of the tiles this afternoon and they all fell off.

Monday July 13th

I've been laughed and/or smirked at four times now for wearing my mask in supermarkets. It's almost as if my fellow subjects are so brimming with British Common Sense that the idea of caring about anyone but themselves is simply hilarious.

Tuesday July 14th

Priceless advice on Good Morning Britain today.

"If you're going to keep a snake as a pet, choose a non-venomous species."

People up and down the country are cancelling their orders for Death Adders and Taipans.

Saturday July 18th

Grant Schapps has just admitted that the Government are no longer following The Science. He said, "I have had meetings with The Scientists and they're all saying they have no idea what this virus has up its sleeve. And therefore we, your elected leaders, are making the rules. And what we say goes. And we're actually experts. Not that anyone needs experts. And we know more about it than them. And anyway, we've vanquished COVID-19. And Rule Britannia. And Brexit. And get back to work you idle bastards. And God Save the Queen. And the Battle of Britain. And Sunny Uplands. And Land of Hope and Glory. And that."

The U.S. death toll passed 145,000 today.

Sunday July 19th

Trump: I think we have one of the lowest mortality rates in the world. Many of those cases are young people that would heal in a day. They have the sniffles, and we put it down as a test.

Me: I think that when I go to the dentist and I'm told that I need a filling, it's not because I went to the dentist. It's because I needed a fucking filling.

Monday July 20th

Today I hoovered the house from top to bottom and smell faintly of good, honest sweat. Sometimes I long for the days when I smelled strongly of immoral, dastardly sweat.

Tuesday July 21st

According to Johnson, we do not have long to wait before we hear the Government's decision on reducing the two metre social distancing rule. People are suffering, but businesses are suffering more.

Trump has now asked that US COVID-19 testing be slowed down. His logic is that fewer tests equal fewer cases. And that makes him look good. As if we didn't know, we can now add Narcissist to his hideous pantheon of failings as a functioning human being.

Wednesday July 22nd

You are at a remote railway station very late at night. It is softly raining, and the only sound is the water drip-drip-dripping from the rust-pocked guttering. You are the only passenger waiting for the last train. You stand, hands in greatcoat pockets, beneath the Victorian station canopy.

Perhaps you are smoking a cigarette, the smoke pluming then hanging in the gently falling rain. In the distance you hear the querulous whistle of a steam train. A steam train? Surely not! It must have been the call of some night creature. The antique rattle of slowly approaching carriages comes ever nearer. The wet, rusted tracks tremble very slightly. You see something huge and skull-like amid the dark and the hissing steam, and the growling of its wheels begins to slow. You narrow your eyes because you can't quite make out the massive shape that is coming to rest before you. Thomas the Tank Engine has pulled up. His face is vast and sneering. "Get on." he bellows, his voice like thunder.

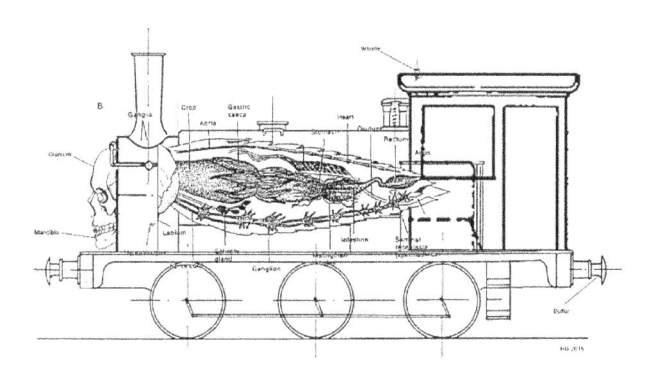

Thursday July 23rd

Domestic abuse cases are going through the roof. I am not, on the whole, all that keen on men. I have spent much of my life working in predominantly male environments. And in my long and painful experience, many men, especially when not in the company of women, are repugnant. Their 'banter' is violent, misogynistic and frequently veers into paedophilic illegality. It is all about fear, power and control. Everyone should be safe from abuse at this time. And always.

People are apparently confused about face-coverings. They are compulsory in all shops from tomorrow. This is like the confusion when free plastic shopping bags became 5p each. That concept was overwhelmingly perplexing as well. I can't believe we live amongst these people. Then again, I can. They voted for the biggest own goal in history because they didn't like all them funny furriners jabbering away on the bus. And they still think it's a brilliant idea.

400,000 passport applications are in backlog. Where in the hell do they think they're going?

Friday July 24th

While walking Jack this morning, I was startled by about fifteen wood pigeons and maybe ten jackdaws taking sudden flight from a flat-roofed outbuilding to the side one of the houses we were going past. This house has a front garden consisting of foot-high grass, weeds, lumps of wood, a skateboard, stolen road signs and, oddly, an old children's rocking horse.

I stopped our walk and watched these birds flying around until I noticed a face leering out of a downstairs window at me, the owner of which was gesticulating wildly and obviously saying something. I gestured to my ear and mouthed that I couldn't hear.

A woman flung the front door open, looking like the grandmother from the Addams Family, and shrieked,

"Keep your fucking dog away from our lawn!! Dogs piss and shit all over it and other dogs can smell it!!"

I brandished my very full dog-poo bag and responded,

"Well, to be fair you don't have a lawn. And we're nowhere near your garden. This is a public footpath. I was looking at the jackdaws and pigeons."

"I feed them." she yelled.

I replied, "That's great! There's no need to be so nasty though."

"There's no need to be so ignorant!!" she screamed, slamming the door.

And we continued our morning walk.

For context, the man this woman is shacked up with wheedled up to me while I was doing an animal rights fundraiser in Glastonbury some years ago.

Him: "You animal rights lot should be more bothered about people!"

Me: "Okay then. What have you done for people lately?"
Him: "Don't you get aggressive with me!"

Me: "You'll know if I'm getting aggressive my friend."

Gyms, venues and theatres reopened today. God help them all.

Saturday July 25th

"We can't call blackberries blackberries anymore!"
"We'll have to call brownies something different!"

Just two of the hilarious statements I have heard from the truly enlightened today.

Sunday July 26th

I sat in the back garden this afternoon constantly sneezing, itching and scratching. If I am made redundant in October, once Sunak's furlough scheme ends, I'm considering opening Somerset's first Allergy Garden.

And I've just realised that there are no cheese-flavoured drinks.

Monday 27th July

Today I started picking up other people's dog shit while I'm out with Jack because I am pig sick of treading in it and having to jump over it. There is an unspoken mantra in this country that *Someone Else Will Do It*. In our cossetted lives, where food standards, Health & Safety Regulations and the NHS are in place to protect us from ourselves, where do we need to take any actual responsibility? Well, our pets for a start. They are our animals. We bought them. They live in our homes. We feed them. We walk them. And it is our responsibility to clear their faeces off the pavements. Disgustingly, a lot of people are incapable of doing this, because *Someone Else Will Do It*. And, it seems, that *Someone* is me at the moment. Apart from being foul, dog muck can contain

Toxocariasis. It can blind people. Still, *Someone Else Will Do It*. In addition, I've started having to wear a mask on my morning walk with Jack, mainly because of joggers. What is the problem with joggers? Every morning I have to either scarper up somebody's driveway or drag the dog onto a main road to avoid their sweaty breath. Are they like trains? Only able to maintain a given trajectory? Are they on fucking rails?

Thursday 30th July

Top Tip!

Don't run out of briefs in a heatwave. The substitute ladies' underwear, whilst highly elegant, has its gusset in exactly the right position to create the ambient gonad temperature of a freshly baked potato.

Friday 31st July

Local lockdown was probably tightened somewhere or other today. Or relaxed. I have no idea. Neither do the Government.

AUGUST 2020

Saturday August 1st

The Government announced today that shielding is going to end. I assume this is people like my Mum, who are elderly or vulnerable. I don't really understand. My mother's generation, the generation most at risk, aren't generally working. So why end shielding? Do they just want to finish them off like they did in Care Homes?

Dr Anthony Fauci, over in the States, has suggested that the reason behind his country's dire COVID-19 performance is that they never actually locked down. "Wrong!" says Trump. "We have more cases because we have tested far more than any other country!" Makes you wonder why there's no 'wanker' emoji.

Sunday August 2

COVID-19 cases are soaring to such an extent that a major incident was announced in Greater Manchester today. And still the Tories are patting themselves on the back about their triumphant efforts. Well done chaps. Have a pheasant. What what!

First sleep concluded at three of the clock. Fed Pimple and Scruffings with the rancid tongue left from Thursday's Barnstaple Society Meeting. Summoned Calvin for elvers, scole and ham, which repast I enjoyed in the soiling chamber. After attending His Majesty, penned two letters to Aloysious McLarkin and Sir Romphrey concerning sentences. Scurrilous performance of Wycherley's "The Intrepid Governers" at The Royal Court. Then by log to Newham for chess. Carousing at The Monk's Udder where young Sir Kenneth Swerries did scrub his manhood against a fair piglet. And so to bed.

Monday August 3rd

The commercials for a month-long "Eat Out to Help Out" scheme have started. It's masked chefs preparing all sorts of sizzling dishes, and there's a 50% discount on meals eaten in indoor venues. The balance of the cost will be picked up by the government. It isn't, though, applicable to takeaways or outdoor eating, both of which are patently less hazardous. If we are to believe that the whole thing is really to "help out" struggling businesses, rather than a PR stunt, why on earth are takeaways not included? These Government TV adverts are trumpeting "Wheeeee we're all back to normal get out there and socialise and spend your money Wheeeeee...". Jesus. This is either woefully premature or deeply sinister. Probably both.

Friday August 7th

I took Jack out quite late tonight. On the way back from our walk I was suddenly yanked back. When regained my balance I realised that, for the first time in nearly 12 years, he had laid down on the footpath. He was looking back the way we'd come. And then he started rolling around.

I looked back. And Cloud came out of the gloom.

Obviously, it wasn't Cloud. It was her doppelgänger. A Husky called Freya. She looks like Cloud though, in every aspect. Apart from a slightly shorter tail. She is the same size. She has the same eyes, same colouring, same gait. She behaves just like Cloud as well, so we had a proper cuddle. Her owner is a nice woman who moved here two months ago. I needed a bloody good cry when I got home.

Sunday August 9th

The daily figure of new COVID-19 infections has passed 1,000 for the first time since June. This isn't all that surprising, considering the half-baked advice from the Government and the obnoxious and bovine behaviour of The Great British Public we've been seeing.

I was reminded by my Mum today that, when I was four, I used to walk around our cottage looking at the reflection of the ceiling in a hand-mirror. I'd 'walk around' light fittings, 'step over' the tops of doors and 'avoid' the chimney breast. It was great fun until I 'fell down' the fucking stairs.

Wednesday August 12th

I heard the perfect response to the idea of Herd Immunity on the radio today. The Government, I sincerely believe, holds this concept at the heart of its decisions. An eminent professor of immunology said, with a knowing smile in her voice, "Well sure, herd immunity is fine if you're happy with thousands of hospital admissions and deaths. And it also helps if there's some guarantee of the key 'immunity' part. Which there isn't."

Thursday August 13th

Kids' A Level grades were announced in Britain today. Over a third of the results were at least a grade lower than their teachers expected. The teachers have been screaming about this for months. How on earth can you use a bloody algorithm to determine someone's whole future? Once again, those Registered Charity schools (Eton, Harrow, Rugby etc) appear to be unaffected. I suspect that the kids who don't go to Registered Charity Schools will start righteously screaming now too. Good.

Friday August 14th

It was announced yesterday that, as of now, all British people returning from France, the Netherlands and a few other places will have to quarantine for two weeks to avoid spreading the virus. Thousands of holidaymakers are frantically sprinting to return to the UK from France before quarantine restrictions begin. While I understand that it's short notice, thanks to the Government, it's this selfless attitude about the health and wellbeing of anyone other than themselves that has made this country what it is today.

And we now have the highest COVID-19 infection rate today than at any time since June. I wonder why.

Saturday August 15th

Some restaurants and pubs said today that they have dropped out of the Eat Out to Help Out scheme because of hostility towards staff. The owners of these establishments have found themselves unable to cope with these swarms of rude and entitled people. One landlady said that she and her staff had experienced nothing but negativity from customers taking advantage of the scheme. Another restaurateur stated that he and his employees have had to put up with extreme levels of rudeness, a lack of understanding, scant regard for COVID-19 safety and complete impatience from his Eat Out to Help Out clientele. So he's packing it in.

Monday August 17th

The education gap between rich and poor kids just got wider because of the COVID-19 pandemic. That's like saying Napolean is more dead now than he was in 1950.

Being honest with myself, with possible redundancy looming, with the world insane and with this relatively aimless and untethered life, I'm now struggling.

Far too much booze.
Far too much grinding anxiety.
Far too little sleep.
Sometimes it's like an all-body-and-soul sag.

Last night I somehow slept for thirteen hours, so I'm no longer fatigued. But the other issues are still very much in evidence. That's life right now I suppose.

Tuesday August 18th

Education Secretary Gavin Williamson said today that he is "incredibly sorry" for the life-destroying nightmare he and his strategies have put children through. Sorrow. He can turn it on and off like a tap.

Wednesday August 19th

France has made the wearing of face coverings compulsory for most places of work. Hancock and Johnson grumbled about it. It's still un-British. There are no plans to legislate for anything so crazily Gallic or utterly lifesaving here.

Linzi gave me a Calippo earlier and I had my first ice-cream headache for several decades. I'd forgotten all about ice-cream headaches. What the fuck is all that about?

Tuesday August 25th

I was playing with Jack tonight and took his collar off. He likes being in the nude from time to time. Looking at his bare neck I realised that the collar isn't "his" at all. It's mine. If I want to take it from him I can. All our animals really have is themselves and us. And in many situations, usually with farmed animals, we take everything that is that animal away. We take their milk, children, muscles, skin, fur, fat, bones, organs, lives. I had never thought about it before. It makes me sad.

Wednesday August 26th

There are a lot of conversations at work, and emails flying about, regarding how on earth my department are supposed to continue. We who have been furloughed aren't contributing anything to the company anymore, and with the scheme ending soon I can only see redundancy as an option.

Prezzo and Harvester, amongst other larger outfits, announced today that they plan to continue the Eat Out to Help Out scheme into next month due to its success. They'll even fund the 50% shortfall themselves if they need to. I assume that they can afford bouncers to protect the staff from the customers.

Johnson has blamed a mutant algorithm, whatever that is, for the exam grades fiasco. These people are amazing. They have never made a miss-step or error in their lives. To a man and woman their truth is incontrovertible. They are deities. Bronzed & Infallible British Gods.

Thursday August 27th

The UK Government in Two Sentences:

1. For fucks sakes stop worrying about the "pandemic" and get out there and work and eat half price fast food.
2. Lose weight so COVID-19 won't kill you, you fat, lazy bastards.

Today, new COVID-19 cases in the UK rose by 1,522, the highest case rate since June. Again.

Friday August 28th

Today I had a major Skype meeting with my CEO and our HR lady. It was quite moving, as we all agreed that there is no way I can do my job. My CEO said that, as and when things get back to something approaching normal, he'll be on the phone asking me to come back. I have worked here for over thirteen years. But, right now, it is impossible. I have agreed on voluntary redundancy as the least painful way to say goodbye, for everyone concerned. It's sad but it was inevitable.

The Government announced that their latest scam to persuade people back into workplaces will begin next week. Why? Especially as BBC Newsnight reported tonight that they have a SAGE document which says that a reasonable worst-case-scenario will result in 85,000 COVID-19 deaths this coming winter?

Saturday August 29th

Nearly August Bank Holiday. We're preparing for the mass of absolute cocks descending on Glastonbury this weekend.

Sunday August 30th

COVID-19 cases in the UK now stand at 334,467 and the total number of fatalities is 41,499. We still have the highest death rate in the whole of the continent. I suppose it makes up for all those Eurovision Song Contests.

Monday August 31st (Summer Bank Holiday)

Well, knock me down! Over 100 Million meals were eaten during the pitiful Eat Out to Help Out scheme. It cost the UK taxpayer around £522 Million. A study has shown (and you might wish to take a seat) that some areas with a high Eat Out to Help Out uptake had increased COVID-19 infections after a week, and that between 8% and 17% of new infections can be linked to the scheme.

It will be a while before we go out again. Especially after Eat Out to Help Out. But when we do, I'm secreting a small piece of scaffolding pipe down my trousers. As the night gets wilder, I'm going to start tapping the pipe with a nut hammer, creating the illusion that I'm wearing a chastity belt. At this point I'm going to sit back and watch all the young men boogie for my favours.

We stayed at home today. Apparently the town was teeming with halfwits.

SEPTEMBER 2020

Tuesday September 1st

Schools in England, Wales and Northern Ireland reopened today.

Low-income workers were suddenly required to self-isolate in those parts of the UK where COVID-19 rates are high. People who can't work from home are now entitled to a new payment scheme to top their Universal Credit claims for the duration of this isolation. This begs the question If Now Why Not Then? We would probably all be back to normal by now. Sickening short-sightedness.

Companies like mine, who are using the Government's furlough scheme, now have to contribute towards their employee's wages.

Testosterone Injection! I got Nurse Ally today. I like Nurse Ally. She spent all of the time before, during and after the injection convincing me that I was doing okay and that all her patients are as fat as fuck right now.

Thursday September 3rd

Baroness "Dido" Harding of Wherever, head of the NHS Test and Trace System, apologised today after it emerged that, because of her incompetence, British laboratories are unable to keep up with demand for

COVID-19 tests. Added to which, people, some of them in the vulnerable category, are being asked to travel several hundred miles to get tested.

One of those Scarab Minor road-sweeper-hoover trucks came past today. They go all over the town, but they have to stop and change the bag twice on our road.

Friday September 4th

Don't laugh, but Johnson ruled out introducing COVID-19 tests at airports today. He says they'd be used to shorten the length of time people are required to quarantine and would give people a false sense of security. Surely anyone in an airport already has a false sense of security?

According to Linzi's 'It's Fate' magazine this month, the way to psychically communicate with your dog or cat is to sit in front of an imaginary TV with an imaginary remote control and flick through imaginary channels until you find one with your pet on it. I had a go at it, but I kept getting Pebble Mill at One.

Monday September 7th (Unemployment Day)

Well. That's it.

I'm redundant.

I'm going to get very, very drunk for a few days and then decide what the hell I'm going to do with the rest of my life.

It's nobody's fault, any of this, unless we want to point the finger at our baleful Government, which I do. I'm certainly not culpable and neither is my company, who went and continue to go well over the odds to do the right thing. I'll genuinely miss them. But it was like a carpenter trying to do his job without a ready supply of wood. Just impossible. At 56 I doubt that many people will be queuing up to offer me a job.

Tuesday September 8th

The Health Secretary, Hancock, told the House of Commons today that the sharp rise in COVID-19 cases is concerning, and that the COVID-19 virus remains a threat. Such insight! It was like listening to Sherlock Holmes or Stephen Hawking. And guess what? Gatherings of more than six people will be banned in England from Monday.

Wednesday September 9th

Today was a bit like a death. When my Dad died it was more-or-less mythical until I saw the coffin. And then it was real. I cleared out my little office today. It's now empty of all of my work items of thirteen years. Now it's real. I am out of work.

Thursday September 11th

We found a drone in the bin at the park today. It was slightly damaged, and we nearly took it home to fix it, but in the end we put it back in the hive.

Sunday September 13th

We had our first socially distanced pint or two in Beckets Inn for ages today. Apart from the bit where I forgot all about social distancing and tried to hug Karen, it was marvellous. And now we await our first curry for seven months to be delivered from the Eliachi. Why not? I've got nothing else to do.

Monday September 14th

Something called "The Rule of Six" has come into force. I can only imagine this is Johnson's attempt to be even more baroque and Victorian than usual by referencing Conan Doyle.

I'm going back to bed now because I've been up since 5am for no reason.

Tuesday September 15th

Not doing so well. More drinking. More sitting aimlessly in the garden. Today's soundtrack: The Jesus Lizard, Julie London, XTC and Siiiii, when I was drunk enough.

First sleep concluded at four fifteen of the clock. Curled wig with lard and hot posset. Summoned Pumper for cockles, barleycorn and chavender, which repast I enjoyed in the gablet. After attending His Majesty, penned two letters to Bishop Llewellyn and Lord Henrick regarding the peeling of swans. Glistering performance of Twelfth Night at The Royal Court. Then by foxhound to Greenwich for the mocking of the afflicted. Carousing in The Popped Vagrant where The Earl of Hackney did pick at his scabs until he was roundly garrotted to death by mine host Vince. And so to bed.

Wednesday September 16th

Johnson appeared in front of a committee of MPs today, saying that a second national lockdown would have 'disastrous financial consequences' for the UK, and that the Government have done 'everything in our power' to avoid that scenario. Eat Out to Help Out was an avoidance tactic then? Who knew?

Today. More garden-sprawling. More Day-Boozing. I need to get a grip. I'm just not sure what I'm supposed to be getting a grip on exactly.

Thursday September 17th

Tonight we took Jack past that house with the jackdaws, pigeons and the rocking horse in the garden. The lady of the house, the one who had called me ignorant for walking a dog on a footpath back in June, was carting something from their Transit van into the house when she spied us. The resulting debacle went something like this:

HER: WHEEEURGH!! I have TOLD you to keep your fucking dog off my garden!
ME: We're nowhere near your garden.
HER (coming so close to my face that I can smell her fetid breath and feel her spittle hitting my face): You. Are. Standing. ON. MY FUCKING. LAWN!
ME: No. We are not.
HER (still in my face): You let your dog shit all over our garden!!
LINZI (brandishing some dog-poo bags): We always pick up after our dog.
HER (glaring past me, with our noses almost touching, at Linzi): No you don't. You just SMEAR IT ABOUT!!
ME: Can you get out of my face? There's a Global Pandemic going on.
HER: Why? Are you going to HIT ME??
ME: Erm… no.
LINZI: Let's go Paul.
HER (as we turn to go): Yes. That's it. Walk away, LITTLE BOY!

At this point the man of the house smarmed out of the front door.

HIM: I'm calling the police because you (pointing at me) RAPED ME LAST WEEK!!

ME: What??

HIM: Yeah. You raped me twice and beat me up three times.

LINZI: Come on. Let's go.

Which we did.

HIM, very loudly and brandishing a mobile phone: HELLO!! POLICE!! YES, THERE'S A MAN HERE WHO RAPED AND ASSAULTED ME LAST WEEK.

We carried on our walk with Jack while this man screamed our descriptions into his mobile. Having spent the last few working weeks prior to my redundancy calling every single constabulary in Britain, I am fully aware that, even after the two-minute recorded COVID-19 preamble, it takes at least another five minutes to speak to anyone. And there is no way he would have called 999 because he would face serious questions about wasting the emergency services' time. But let's be honest. He's a twat and he didn't phone anyone.

When we got home I was furious. It's not as if I don't have quite enough on my plate right now. I emailed our local police about them. What the hell makes these people think for a moment that the path outside their non-existent lawn is some sort of fiefdom? I am also concerned that this random harpy was spitting in my face during a bloody pandemic.

Dido Harding has told MPs that demand for COVID-19 testing is significantly outstripping the capacity she has put in place. Again. She is, though, "very confident" that daily testing capacity will be up to 500,000 by the end of October. From zero to 500,000 in two weeks?

Today just kept getting better and better.

Friday September 18th

There is Government COVID-19 news today, but I simply cannot be bothered to write about it. Imagine a gang of toddlers trying to escape from a burning playgroup with their lives while simultaneously needing to rescue their favourite toys. Which are already on fire.

Sleep is more difficult now than at any time of my life. After about three hours of it on Thursday, I doused myself with hearty liquor yesterday after all the weirdness, and triumphantly went up at 8pm. Then again at about 10pm. Again at 11.45pm. And again at 1am. It's horrible. I guess this is to be expected during the End of Days.

And I got an emergency COVID-19 test after the intimacy with the scum of the earth last night. I'm virus free, but tested positive for foot and mouth, hookworm, BSE, scrapie, anthrax and scrofula.

Saturday September 19th

As well as the police, I have now also been in contact with the YOU RAPED ME! people's Housing Association. The police have opened an incident report on them, and the Housing Association are as bloody useless as I expected. We now refer to them as The Hedgers. Because they deserve to live in a hedge. Far, far away from anyone civilised.

Boffin News! Robert Dingwall, Professor of Sociology at Nottingham Trent University, says that there is growing public support for a complete re-evaluation of the government's strategy for dealing with the COVID-19 pandemic as scientific knowledge of the virus increases.

Monday September 21st

We walked Jack near the psychotic Hedger House tonight and were beckoned over by Athena and Athena, a couple who live next door to them who happen to have the same name. What are the odds? I'd chatted to these two quite a lot before all of these shenanigans, but for some reason hadn't put two-and-two together regarding the Hedger's possible impact on them as neighbours. They heard the shrieking on Thursday and said that they are absolutely toxic. Not only do they regale these women with homophobic abuse almost daily, but the big brave man of the house gets off by being aggressive to the pensioners from the sheltered housing apartments across the way. Athena and Athena asked us "not to hold back" because they are a nightmare to live next to. Armed with information I am now awaiting a further telephone call from The Fuzz. The Hedgers will rue the day. I now have something to focus on, and my errant mind is thus slightly calmer.

Dr Patrick Vallance, the UK government's chief scientific adviser, said today that there could be as many as 50,000 COVID-19 cases per day by mid-October if no further action is taken, and that this "would be expected to lead to about 200 deaths per day".

Tuesday September 22nd

The Great British Public, demonstrating once more their innate common sense and empathy, have begun clearing the supermarket shelves again.

In a televised address, Johnson called for people to "exercise discipline and resolve" to combat COVID-19. He warned that further measures may be required if they don't adhere to the restrictions. The only resolve we've seen is people 'resolving' to buy every toilet roll in Tesco. Feather the nest and fuck the rest eh, Boris? It's the Tory way after all.

Wednesday September 23rd

6,178 new COVID-19 cases today. The highest daily number recorded since May 1st.

Asda announced today that it will introduce tougher measures to enforce the wearing of face coverings by its customers. Imagine the 'discipline and resolve' being displayed by their customers for them to make this a necessity.

Thursday September 24th

Oh brilliant! Rather than ending the furlough scheme as he's been trumpeting for months, Sunak announced today that they're just changing its name to "The Job Support Scheme". This starts on 1 November and is open-ended as far as I can see. Just great. I am redundant from a job of thirteen years for absolutely no reason. Cheers Rishi. This Government couldn't run a fucking bath.

Friday September 25th

I spent much of today spiralling from the reality that I would still have a job, albeit on a diminished salary, if not for the ham-fisted and Three Stooges-like actions of our Leaders.

It feels like I'm losing control. I know these feelings are temporary. And I know I'm not the only person living this anchorless nightmare. Every night seems epic. The throwing of food into the mouth. The pleasantries. The news. The getting up. The moving around. Extra snacks, maybe with peanut butter. More endless, endless news. The decision to turn in, then not. Because something else has appeared on the news. The realisation that you cannot stay up. The knowledge that you could fall over at any point just reaching the top of the stairs. The soft sanctuary of bed. The restless, revolving silence. The failing effort to fall into the refuge of sleep.

September 26th

Thousands of protesters gathered in Trafalgar Square today for a COVID-19 anti-restrictions-and-lockdown protest. The demonstration was eventually shut down by police due to those attending not adhering to social distancing.

Monday September 28th

I came across Linzi doing something underhand near the ironing board in the living room today. I'd like to know what gives the female half of the population the right to go through the male half's comfy, beloved, perfectly serviceable but elderly pants, socks and t shirts and chuck them in the bin 'because they look horrible now'.

My redundancy package came through today. A bittersweet event. I cleared all our debts. I ordered a new mattress because ours has had it. And I paid for my cremation. I have no desire for a funeral. Funerals, in my experience, are dreary events. My friend Daryl Martin's at the age of thirteen was enough to put me off for life. Added to which, the Church can't be trusted. I wrote a lengthy eulogy for my father's funeral, my reading of which was vetoed for some reason. The Methodist Minister who was conducting the ceremony, though, came to my mother's house one afternoon while I was there and asked for my preliminary notes so she could expand and elaborate on them in line with, I imagine, Jesus, God and so on. On the day of my Dad's funeral, she stood in her clerical collar and just read my incomplete jottings verbatim. Errors and all. It was vile and lazy and totally lacked respect. I want nothing of the sort. I have paid a company called Pure Cremation to collect my carcass from wherever it ends up, ignite me, shovel what's left into a cremulator (for the teeth) and deliver the resulting grey gravel back here. Then I'm getting chucked around up Glastonbury Tor with the grass and cows and sheep and pagans. Then, if the pubs are open, I want my friends get outrageously drunk at Beckets Inn listening to The Specials and Grandaddy.

Tuesday September 29th

It's now a month or so since this enforced feckless existence. And I am surely chipping away at what is left of my Goodbye Money. But, right this minute, what else is there?

I bought a 12 String Guitar today. Second hand. From a nice man near Meare whose enormous house looked like a stage-set. I have always wanted one. It sounds gorgeous but I'm not entirely sure what to I'm going to do with the thing.

7,143 new COVID-19 cases today, with 71 COVID-19 deaths. The highest since 1st July. Johnson, THIS is what you call World Beating.

Wednesday September 30th

Johnson held one of his briefings at Downing Street. He said that the 'Rule of Six' measures he introduced two weeks previously will take time to feed through. Time is the one luxury we never have a species when we are confronted with incurable diseases. Timely intervention, however, is. And that is the one thing we haven't seen in this country for nearly a year. It's those toddlers again, trying to protect their precious blazing toys while scurrying to save themselves. And, as with toddlers worldwide, they care not one iota about anyone but themselves.

Imagine the scene. It is 1470. My Lady has a Dermal Plague, acquired from her hawk's talons. This malady has taken hold, too, in her lady's maid and her seamstress. My Lady requires dry warmth and a poultice. Whilst not a proven cure, a poultice of blue clay and bread may help her, and thence her two maidservants and mayhap the court entire, recover from the sickness.

Courtier: Oh Surgeon! My Lady fails. She sweats and shakes, and the wound suppurates. She begs for a poultice, Doctor, to sooth and, if God wills, heal her.

Surgeon: Sir, I have prepared such a treatment and shall attend My Lady forthwith.

Sir Matthew Hand of Cock: Hang about… let's just fanny around for a few weeks while we make some dosh eh? After all, money talks and bullshit walks!

Lord Borrisington of Twat: (unintelligible)

Courtier: But Sir Matthew! Lord Borrisington! She will surely fail unto death.

Surgeon: Yes. Sirs! I pray you allow me to practice my craft for it may save her and, God-willing, countless more poor souls.

Sir Matthew Hand of Cock: … Nah.

OCTOBER 2020

Thursday October 1st

Jeremy Corbyn has issued an apology after being photographed hosting a dinner-party with more than six people sitting around the dinner table. Stanley Johnson has issued an apology after he was pictured in a shop without a face covering. I'm racking my brain here figuring out which of these two equally egregious faux pas will get the most column inches in the British press.

SNP MP, Margaret Ferrier, was suspended from her party today. She took a train from her Scottish constituency to London, contravening COVID-10 restrictions. She has publicly stated that there was "no excuse" for her behaviour. She should have had a word with Dominic Cummings. He had fucking loads.

Friday October 2nd

TRUMP HAS COVID!! Or has he?

Saturday October 3rd

Jack has crapped on the landing two nights this week. I've just spent half an hour in the garden clearing up the culprits behind this unholy hell. About sixty unripe and over-ripe tomatoes had fallen off the plants when I finally binned them, and I didn't notice them. He's been out there eating them for bloody days.

Sunday October 4th

The cinema chain Cineworld is shutting for a while, and Hancock is bringing in the Army to help distribute the COVID-19 vaccine. I didn't know there was a vaccine.

Monday October 5th

We spoke to the Athenas tonight. The Hedgers are still at it. And now they're terrorising Mums with toddlers. And sub-letting.

When we returned home, I penned this email to their Housing Association: "As I haven't heard from you for a fortnight, I thought I would bring you up to date with your poisonous tenants' behaviour. We actually thought they had stopped harassing people walking by your rental property as we had not seen them for a while, but, according to their neighbours, not only have they been renting your property out as an Air B&B, but have also been intimidating mothers with four-year-old children who have the audacity to use the public footpath outside your property by screaming in their faces, at a time of global pandemic, in broad daylight. We can add the above to the harassment of passing pensioners and the homophobic abuse their neighbours experience daily. This has also been logged with Avon & Somerset Police."

As ever with Housing Associations though, I fear that their benefit-system rent will trump any legal or moral considerations.

In other news, Public Health England, the Government's Deception Wing of the British medical profession, confirmed that all of those involved in the delayed reporting of daily COVID-19 cases have now been contacted. Unfortunately, the delay has meant that all of the people they came into contact with haven't. Hancock made a statement to the effect that, although this was an error, it wasn't an error.

Following Sunday's closure announcement from Cineworld, Johnson has started urging people to go to the cinema.

Trump still reckons he has COVID-19, and there's a weird global outpouring of best wishes for him. I'm supposed to find out that the most disgusting, repugnant excuse for a human being I have ever seen polluting the world stage has contracted a virus he has been laughing about for months and 'wish him well'? I'm with the virus on this one.

Tuesday October 6th

We walked Jack near the Hedger House, and the Athenas next door told us that the police have been round and had a long word with them. We carried on past the Hedger House. Mr Hedger took one look at me through the window and immediately averted his eyes.

And we saw the most incredible video! Trump swaggered out of the Walter Reed National Military Medical Center in Washington yesterday after, apparently, defeating COVID-19. He was filmed on a balcony of the White House after his return, where he stood, looking like a Poundland Demigod. Then he removed his face mask with a flourish, before giving a military salute to a load of random helicopters that were disappearing into the sunset. It was like Apocalypse Now! This whole fiasco was accompanied by stirring martial music and almost Spielberg-like cinematography. I have never seen anything as self-aggrandising or desperate in my life. It was hysterical.

Wednesday October 7th

My previously-local Bury St Edmunds-based pub company and brewer Greene King announced the loss of 800 jobs, saying lockdown is to blame. They've closed about 80 pubs and say that about 25 of them will never open again.

Thursday October 8th

The Office for National Statistics say that there were three times more deaths from COVID-19 than from flu and pneumonia combined between January and August 2020. Three times. The 'oh it's only like the flu' brigade are eerily silent about this.

Is it just me or do Potus and Flotus sound like a couple of penguins from a Disney Pixar movie?

Friday October 9th

Sunak announced an expansion of the Job Support Scheme today. Furloughed people will have two-thirds of their salaries paid by the Treasury. While I'm happy for everyone benefiting from this, I am also bloody seething.

Saturday October 10th

The British Medical Association has published a list of recommendations to reduce COVID-19 infections. These include the wearing of face coverings in all workplaces, shops, and outdoors where you can't be two metres away from other people. Well, that's everywhere. I'm thinking about inventing some sort of lethal, spinning six-foot blade on a rotor to keep these people the fuck away from me. Nothing else seems to work.

I've been trying to think of a title for my solo album if I ever complete it. The best I've come up with so far is "Monkeywank".

Sunday October 11th

Linzi and I just had a quick cuddle in the kitchen. It got quite romantic at one point, and I began to gently sing in her ear.

Jack came in and began to vigorously and loudly shag my right leg. The lads came down to see what all the racket was. Linzi asked me if I was singing the music from a romcom and I told her that it was the Steptoe theme.

I won't be doing that again.

Monday October 12th

From Wednesday, the country is going into something called a "Tier System". There are three tiers, separated according to class. Places like Manchester and Liverpool, which are full of working-class people, are expected to be placed in the highest tier, meaning that they can only leave the bedroom to walk the whippet or tend to the pigeons. The Home Counties will be in the middle tier and will be able to drive their children to violin lessons and pop into Surrey to check on their second-home builds. Residents of wealthy areas such as Chelsea, Kensington and Knightsbridge, in the lowest tier, will be paid handsomely by the Government for having indoor meetings of six or more.

First sleep concluded at two thirty of the clock. Berated Constable Jennings from bedroom window for brazen whistling. Summoned Tobias for pike, bread and quinces, which repast I enjoyed in the priest hole. After attending His Majesty, penned two letters to Lord Ganglion and Sir Peter Cartwright regarding dust. Lacklustre performance of The Scottish Play at The Royal Court. Then by piggyback to Hampstead for "Cricket by Candlelight". Carousing at The Wooden Tooth, where Charles Makepeace soiled himself. And so to bed.

Tuesday October 13th

The SAGE committee has suggested what they describe as a Circuit Breaker be imposed. The idea is for a kind of mini lockdown for a few weeks, so the virus has nowhere to go and fizzles out. Why oh why oh why did the Government not try something like this to begin with? For everyone, not just white-collar workers and the wealthy or people in high risk places? I'll spend the rest of the night pondering that conundrum.

Wednesday October 14th

Today we went to Clarks Village, a huge shopping precinct in the nearby village of Street, for the first time in months. We didn't want to. We had to take something back. There was a one-way system in place, barriers, signs, hand sanitiser, bright yellow footprints painted on the pavement, all so people knew what to do and the direction of flow. I have never felt so susceptible. Nobody was socially distancing and hardly anybody was adhering to the very simple one-way system. It was like being an extra in a zombie moron movie. Both of us had a shower and a change of clothes when we got home. We won't be going back.

Thursday October 15th

There's a double bed sheet attached to the roundabout down the road with one of those 'Happy Birthday so-and-so' things painted on it in black. There are two birthday girls (I assume twins), which is nice. But I spent the weekend questioning the good taste of painting a couple of sperm on there to reflect the Great Moment of Conception. When we drove past it today Linzi told me to shut up because they're actually two party-balloons on strings.

Friday October 16th

I ordered a COVID-19 Test Kit from Imperial College London today. It's part of a survey. Why not?

Saturday October 17th

England is now registering 27,900 new COVID-19 cases a day. That's a whopping 60% up on last week. Meanwhile, in Wales, their Government has imposed a travel-ban on people from UK COVID-19 hotspots. That's basically England from what I can gather.

Sunday October 18th

Note Left for Linzi in the Kitchen Today: Dear Linzi. I know it looks like a dirty protest, but it was an accident.

Monday October 19th

I heard some pretentious tosspot say on the radio this morning that once art becomes mass-produced it "ceases to be art". I believe this was Primrose Hill shorthand for "If you can't afford the original work, you don't deserve the experience". I have two words as a riposte. 'Literature' and 'Music'.

Tuesday October 20th

We exchanged Christmas presents today. I box-framed an ornate corn dolly for Linzi that she had wanted framing for years. It was vital to get it done before all the shops shut again. I painted the frame too, in the shade of matt dark green she asked for. Linzi bought me a Yamaha DD-75 electronic drum kit which doesn't require programming. The way things are going we just thought what the hell? God only knows what the world is going to be like at Christmas, and my redundancy money is running out.

Wednesday October 21st

26,688 new COVID-19 cases were recorded here today. This is the highest daily figure so far.

Thursday October 22nd

Sunak announces yet more financial help for workers affected by COVID-19. Employers now have to pay less, and employees need to work fewer hours, to qualify for this. Again, over a month on from the destruction of my own career, I am simultaneously delighted and livid.

Friday October 23rd

It seems that criminal and bogus COVID-19 Marshals are now visiting people's homes with fake ID to gain entry. They then issue spurious fines or even offer counterfeit tests for money. I wonder who they vote for.

Saturday October 24th

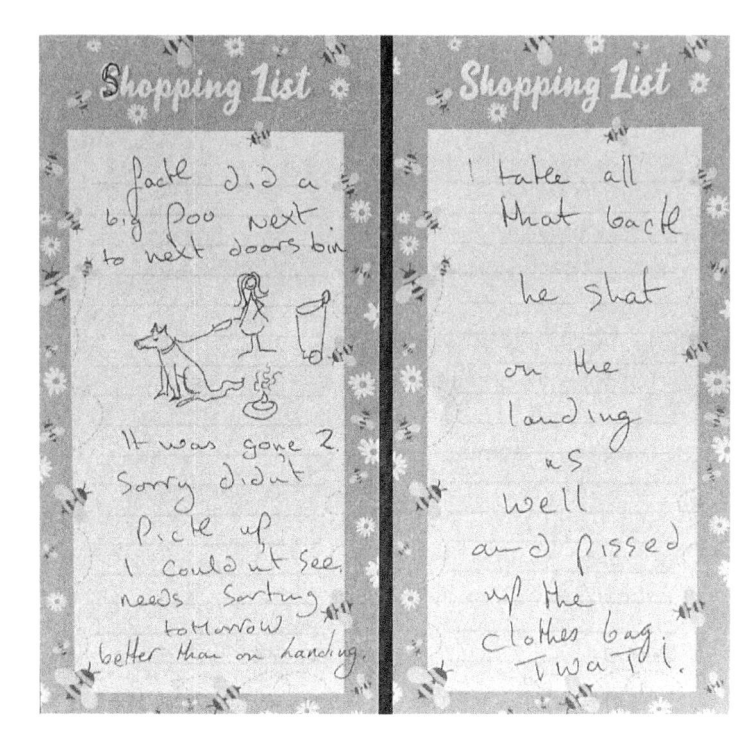

> Jack did a big poo next to next doors bin
>
> It was gone 2. Sorry didnt pick up I couldnt see, needs sorting tomorrow better than on landing.

> I take all that back he shat on the landing as well and pissed up the clothes bag. Twat!

Sunday October 25th

I got so fed up with the gritty feel of the rubbish disposable slippers I've been wearing for years that I popped to the venerable Drapers of Glastonbury to get something decent. The place is amazing. There are lots of little chaps tapping away at workbenches like gnomes, using arcane tools. It smells incredible too. All leathery and old. I bought a pair of handmade leather moccasins, which happened to be on offer. It's like wearing smooth gloves on your feet, rather than sacks full of pea shingle.

We discussed tonight whether it is considered polite to burp after a meal in certain cultures because you're less likely to start farting later in the evening.

Monday October 26th

The UK recorded 367 COVID-19 deaths today, the highest number of daily fatalities since May.

1. I videoed my dog being brilliant on my iPad tonight.
2. I tried to upload it to YouTube.
3. I couldn't upload it to YouTube because I 'hadn't given myself permission' to do so.
4. On trying to rectify this, I was offered the option to watch Gangsta TV, people dressed up for Halloween, or to log out of my account.
5. Turned off computer.

Wednesday October 28th

We watched one of those historical documentaries tonight where they reconstruct some long-dead notable's face with sculptor's clay, using paintings and skull fragments as a guide. Instead of debating what historical figures looked like, why can't we just dig them up and use the whole skulls for facial reconstructions? In fact, we could make certain of the method's accuracy by exhuming recently deceased famous people for whom there is photographic evidence and calibrate the technique. We could do it blind, like a sort of skeletal Generation Game. I'd watch it!

Thursday October 29th

A further statement from Imperial College London suggests there are 100,000 new COVID-19 cases in England every day. Every day! And this number, if the people who are supposed to be running the place don't sort themselves out, will double every nine days. This means that the equivalent of the population of Oldham is becoming infected every day, and if this projection is accurate, by the first week of December, we're looking at the population of Manchester being infected. Every day.

In Trumpaloozaland, he reckons that "if he can recover, anyone can recover." Donald, you didn't have COVID-19 any more than my garden shed did, you vile bastard.

Friday October 30th

We bought some sweets for tomorrow night's Halloween kids. Then we decided we didn't want random people knocking on the door. I stuck a laminated sign on it which reads COVID-19 VULNERABLE! PLEASE DO NOT CALL!!. Then we ate a whole tub of Celebrations and we feel guilty and fat.

Saturday October 31st

Happy Samhain. Happy Halloween. Linzi and I would like to thank Johnson plc for losing me my job for no reason, for not being able to see our Mums since February, for treating blue collar workers and the North of England with contempt, and for needlessly destroying not only thousands of lives but devastating what passed for an economy. Good luck with Brexit you oven-ready bastards.

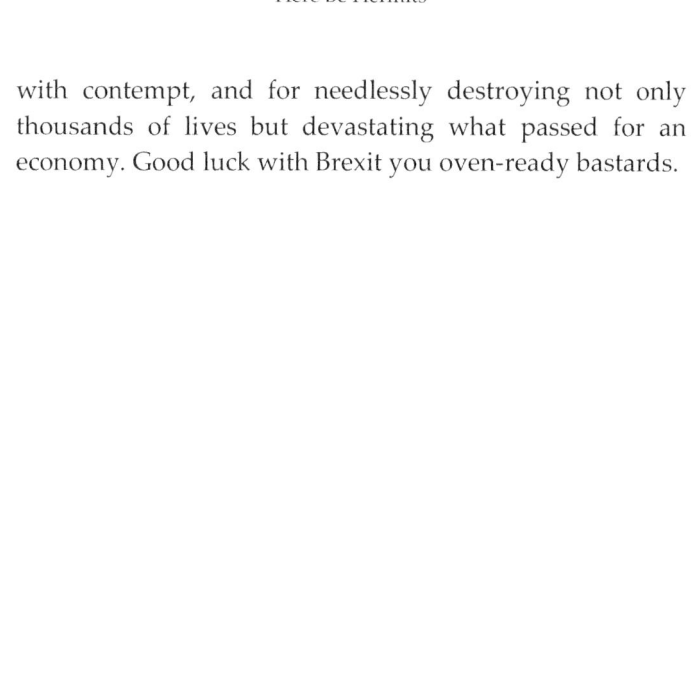

NOVEMBER 2020

Sunday November 1st

At about 9pm last night my sister rang my Mum's landline. The call came through to my mobile which I didn't answer because I was upstairs. On realising she'd reached someone's mobile my sister pressed Last Number Redial and got straight through to my Mum. When I called my sister back to see what she wanted she was really surprised and had no explanation. This is because she doesn't have my mobile number. True Halloween Story!

The results from my Imperial College COVID-19 survey test came back today. I don't have COVID-19 but I do have foot and mouth, hookworm, BSE, scrapie, anthrax and scrofula.

We have our yearly flu-jab at noon today.

Monday November 2nd

Well, that was a nightmare. After feeling okay for a couple of hours after the flu-jab, Linzi disappeared upstairs to bed with a temperature. By about 9pm, having felt gradually hotter and sicker as the afternoon went on, I genuinely believed I was going to die. I made it to the upstairs bathroom, where I locked the door and stripped naked because of the fever. Then I collapsed on the floor and started being sick. I passed out and only came to when I heard distant voices. The lads were outside the door asking if I was alright. There I lay, suffering, unable to move a muscle and moaning. One of them ran downstairs to get a screwdriver so they could get in, and the other one knocked on our bedroom door and got Linzi up. She knocked on the door, not feeling the full ticket herself, and I summoned the strength to lean across the room and unlock the door. She came in, shutting the door behind her. Grabbing a towel, she rubbed the copious sweat from me and coaxed me to my feet. After some staggering about I managed to fall into bed, where I passed out again. In comfort.

Tuesday November 3rd

Woke up this morning feeling fine. Whereas Linzi's still not too good. I know you're supposed to have a mild reaction to vaccines, but this was like being simultaneously buried alive and exhumed. If the vaccine is this bad, what the hell is this year's flu like?

Anyway. US Elections. Here we go. For fucks sakes America, do the right thing. I am absolutely wired about this. He cannot win. No. No. No. A thousand times No.

First sleep concluded at one fifty of the clock. Constructed model of The Bloody Tower from candlewax and blister-water. Summoned Haughley for minnow, sedge and champ, which repast I enjoyed in the Lady Chapel. After attending His Majesty, penned two letters to Sir George Remus and Corkerry regarding trays. Alarming performance of Milton's Fart! at The Royal Court. Then by Galloping Henry to Lambeth for the stoning. Carousing at The Damaged Iris where aged Sir Quincey Drummond was emptied from a barrel, having been drowned therein eight years previously. And so to bed.

Wednesday November 4th

Another 492 COVID-19 deaths today. Yet again the highest number since May. The UK total is now 47,742.

Linzi is beginning to recover from her flu-jab, in that she just has eaten some Heinz Tomato Soup and berated me for asymmetrical buttering of the bread.

Thursday November 5th (Bonfire Night)

LOCKDOWN AGAIN. Or is it?

We're both better after the jab. The UK Statistics Authority, whoever they are, released a statement today criticising the Government over the way daily COVID-19 deaths have been reported. It appears they've been massaging things for PR purposes.

Sunak has now extended the furlough scheme until the end of March next year.

It was my last Testosterone Injection of the year this afternoon. Once I'd got through security, Nurse Helen was hiding behind her door and jumped out at me shouting "Hoy!" when I knocked. I nearly went through the ceiling. She told me I still looked fat, warmed the vial of treacly serum in her armpit for a change (a process I found curiously arousing) and demanded a buttock. After the injection, she managed to stab me in the forearm with the syringe, but it was probably my fault for wildly gesticulating in an NHS facility. The worst thing about going for my injection at the GP's is all the sick people in there. Why can't they all fuck off somewhere else?

Friday November 6th

Linzi didn't get up until gone Noon today. I thought that it was only fair that she had a big lie-in, considering I woke her up throughout the night trying to warm my freezing cold arse on her, and at one point pushed her off the edge of the bed with it.

Hopefully the world is just hours away from a kinder, calmer world once Trump's armed morons get shoved back under their stones.

Saturday November 7th

They did it!! America did it!! Biden and Harris have won. After all the dirty tricks and lawsuits and recounts and lies, all the underhand deals and threats and cajoling and fake news, the fascist lowlife cunt is out of a job. Hallelujah!! I'm setting a rocket off in the back garden later, but first we're getting drunk on Champagne!

I imagine that this will be the point where his aides, advisors and erstwhile colleagues begin to drift away, Thomas-Cromwell-like, for fear of guilt by association. It must be turning into a very lonely and exposed existence for him. What an absolute crying shame.

Jack has started shagging my left leg whenever I laugh at anything. And considering today's events, it's getting a damn good seeing-to tonight.

Sunday November 8th

I'm still buzzing after yesterday, and my American friends are delighted. Criminal proceedings next I hope, once he isn't protected by his office.

Denmark, of all places, has been removed from the UK quarantine exemption. Apparently, the Danish Health Authority have discovered a new strain of COVID-19 in mink. Mink? Are mink running around Denmark spreading their pathogens? So, non-British people can't come to the UK from Denmark. Although why they'd want to come here in the first place is beyond me. We're Europe's Isolation Ward right now.

In Grease, if Frenchie looked like an Easter Egg with all that candy-pink hair, why was it *her* hair that was candy-pink? You don't practice hair dyeing on yourself at Beauty School, do you? Even if you're a drop-out?

Tuesday November 10th

We heard today that the Pfizer and Oxford vaccines are incredibly effective. Could be the first ray of light following Johnson's Travelling Circus. If these vaccines do work, which we don't know, I can't wait for the Tories to start taking the credit. It's like School isn't it, chaps? Brainy Turpin Minor, whose father has to work for a living, did a fine job figuring out what was wrong with that extractor fan in the Senior Common Room. But it was us fellows what basked in the glory, what what? Because we shut the uppity little swine up for the oik he is.

There's also a New Kid in Town. The COVID Recovery Group. It is headed up by somebody called Mark Harper, who is apparently the Tory MP for Forest of Dean. Haunted Victorian Pallbearer Rees-Mogg is involved, inevitably. They are arguing for a set of policies which will allow British society to 'live with the virus'. This is shorthand for 'you lot can live with the virus… we'll be living it up behind our thirty-foot hedges and automatic gates and we'll have you arrested if you try to get in, you fucking plebs.'

Wednesday November 11th

Time to Clap the Government, as the UK becomes only the fifth country on the planet to record 50,000 COVID-related deaths. We're presently trailing the USA, Brazil, India and Mexico but it's all to play for. Go us.

Thursday November 12th

I'm not exactly sure what happened overnight but it feels like I've been kicked in the penis.

Friday November 13th

Kids are now bringing COVID-19 into their households because a new variant is more infectious to young people. This is particularly concerning with multiple-generational homes obviously.

The lads next door turned our shared driveway into a gym earlier today. They began by hitting a car tyre with a mallet one hundred times each. Then they took it in turns tying one end of a rope around their waists, attaching the tyre to the other end, and running up and down the road dragging it behind them while the others stood around hollering encouragement. It was hysterical.

Monday November 16th

The Prime Minister, six Conservative MPs and two political aides are all self-isolating after encountering some Tory MP called Lee Anderson, who later tested positive for COVID-19. All of these worthies were at a Downing Street breakfast meeting four days ago and were, unbelievably, contacted by NHS Test and Trace! Bloody hell, Dido! Having a bad week?

It's already unashamedly Christmas in this house from now on. Daily Festive Channel 5 movies. Advokaat. Chocolates. Scotch. Mulled wine. Mince pies. Sacred Husky.

Tuesday November 17th

At the start of the pandemic, and again in June, a Florida-based jewellery designer called Michael Saiger signed up a Spanish businessman called Gabriel Gonzalez Andersson to act as a go-between to secure PPE for the

NHS . I've read this a few times and still can't really get to grips with it.

The deal was described as "lucrative" by Saiger. I'm not surprised. It cost UK taxpayers £21m.

Wednesday November 18th

I saw a report from the National Audit Office today. The National Audit Office is an independent body that scrutinises public spending for Parliament. They reported that suppliers of PPE with connections to the Tory Party (donors and so on) were 10 times more likely to be awarded contracts. And in a typical response to this, Johnson says he is "proud" of the way the Government secured this equipment. Mind you, if I were in the public eye, I think it would be my life's work to be described as 'disgraced' at least once in my career.

Thursday November 19th

Ten further countries were removed from the UK no-go list today. No countries were removed from the list. Come on Britain! Let's see your money!!

We've put the heating on for the first time this year and the house smells like roasting dust.

Saturday November 21st

People will be allowed to form extended 'Bubbles' to allow them to spend time together over the festive season. While this is nice, it's also incredibly stupid. I imagine the Government will urge caution, but as this will come with a caveat that the Common Sense of The Great British Public will be the key, I predict a massive COVID-19 spike in January.

I have a telephone appointment with Universal Credit on Monday. That'll be an education. I'm not certain who for.

Sunday November 22nd

People are considering taking legal action against the Government over its appointment of old Dido there.

Monday November 23rd

Until today, the Government had shelled out £15billion of our money on Baroness "Dido" Harding of Goodwood's Test & Trace programme. The bill's gone up because they just threw another £7billion at her.

The Universal Credit telephone call was with a lady called Julie at the local Job Centre and she was really pleasant and positive. What on earth has happened since I last had to deal with the benefit system? They used to be grim, sadistic, stony-eyed beasts more suited to hanging off church spires.

Tuesday November 24th

1. Intelligence

Professor Andrew Hayward, a member of the SAGE committee, has warned people to be cautious over Christmas, suggesting the relaxing of rules would be tantamount to "throwing fuel on the COVID-19 fire".

2. Stupidity

The Government announced today that three UK households will be able to meet up indoors or outdoors for the five days between 23rd to 27th December.

I heard one idiot agreeing with this, saying that "isolation is as bad as COVID-19", and that we should all just forget about the pandemic and get together with our families for Christmas. Correct me if I'm wrong, but for the sake of a turkey lunch, won't this inevitably result in thousands of people being in Festive Isolation, in a Festive Wooden Gift Box, under six feet of Festive Mud. Forever?

Talking about food, when we're new-born, all we really are is what our Mums had to eat for the previous nine months.

Wednesday November 25th

696 new COVID-19 deaths in the UK. Once more, that's the highest daily figure since May.

Thursday November 26th

It was announced today that England's new and inexplicable tier system comes into force next Wednesday, and I doubt I'm alone in not knowing what the bloody hell is going on.

Friday November 27th

SAGE issued a document today advising people not to have sleepovers or play board games during Christmas. I know a few people who'd happily come back from beyond the grave to experience a Christmas like that. Including me.

They also suggested that families "involve women in the decision-making process for organising Christmas events, because they carry the burden of creating and maintaining family traditions and activities at Christmas." Same as usual then.

Sunday November 29th

Today was a beautiful day. Whyso? Because Trump's campaign just spent $3Million getting Joe Biden 132 more votes in Wisconsin!

"Jack! For Christ's sake get off my fucking leg!"

We lit our downstairs Festive 'Christmas Berries' Toilet Candle for the first time tonight. Well, I did. We use candles like some people use Febreze.

Monday November 30th

Version Four of The Baroness's COVID-19 Test & Trace is just around the corner. Quite excited. The Baroness. Makes her sound like a Batman villain.

And our local pub can't open because they don't serve food. As is widely understood, COVID-19 runs screaming at the sight of a basket of scampi.

DECEMBER 2020

Tuesday December 1st

ichael Gove popped his little head through The Round Window today to say there are no plans to introduce vaccine passports to ensure that people are safe in places like pubs and restaurants once a vaccine becomes available.

Today I left all the Bigots Talking Shite exposing-everyday-racism social media groups I was in. Not because of anything specific, although the constant use of the word 'gammon' is a little tedious. I've left because being confronted by hatred and filthy stupidity on an hourly basis had started making me very anxious. I have known about this poisonous human garbage for years. It has got far worse since Brexit. And it's gone into the stratosphere since Black Lives Matter became mainstream news. So I'm definitely glad these sites are out there potentially educating people. For myself, though, I need to sleep at night.

Wednesday December 2nd

Blimey! We're the first in the world to approve the Pfizer/BioNTech COVID-19 Vaccine.

Thursday December 3rd

We haven't got an Advent Calendar this year. Instead, we're knocking on doors number one to twenty-five along our road, one a day. Because we only decided to do this at 1am this morning we went out and did numbers one to three. It was a bit disappointing. Rather than a chocolate there was just a really angry bloke in his underpants behind every door.

Friday December 4th

Students can start going home for Christmas today.

60,000 people are dead here now.

Saturday December 5th

A woman with the surname 'Haddock' was on the TV this morning. Intrigued, I looked up the origin of the name. According to one genealogy site it derives from the medieval word Ædduc, a diminutive of Æddi, which is a short form of various compound names including the root ēad, meaning prosperity or fortune. According to another site, one of her ancestors looked like a haddock.

Monday December 7th

The UK's vaccination rollout will begin tomorrow. Sir Simon Stevens, chief executive of NHS England, says that the rollout of the vaccine will be a turning point in the fight against COVID-19. The Government say that most vulnerable people will get their jabs in January and February. Fabulous!

Let's be clear though. The Government just signed the purchase order. It's the NHS who will be doing the work. And they'll be doing it *despite* years of underfunding by the Tories. If they start taking the credit it will be like the wholesaler who supplied paints to Leonardo da Vinci getting recognition for The Mona Lisa.

Matt Hancock was just on the telly and Linzi said "Look at that twat. You can almost see his foreskin twitch." And I cannot for the life of me get this fucking image out of my head.

Tuesday December 8th

A great day! Vaccinations of the Pfizer COVID-19 vaccine get going. A ninety-year-old lady called Margaret Keenan from Coventry gets the first UK jab, and one William Shakespeare, 81 from Warwickshire becomes the second. The Oxford/AstraZeneca COVID vaccine is also considered safe after tests.

In response to this, Hancock auditioned for The Newmarket Scallywags Amateur Dramatic Society on TV this morning, delivering a truly moving rendition of the crying scene from Truly, Madly, Deeply. Critics were astonished by the depth of his performance, while ruminating on the fact that he produced not one single tear throughout. A true master of his craft.

A group of entitled faux hippies have taken up residence on the High Street. They use coloured chalks to write their insane conspiracy theories about the fact that we've all been conned, and nobody has ever really died of COVID-19, all over the pavements outside the church and elsewhere. This one was in three-foot-high pink and green letters outside Tesco today: "COVID 19 IS THE BIGGEST SCAM IN HIS-STORY". Here's an idea! Rather than making the place look like a playgroup, why not volunteer to help out at some local NHS ICU wards? Because the virus is imaginary, you'll not require any PPE. And it would free up NHS staff to deal with patients suffering from 'real' medical conditions. You can do something worthwhile and prove your point simultaneously. It's a Win Win!

Thursday December 10th

1. Massive storm predicted for Somerset tomorrow morning.
2. Woman four doors down puts her wheelie bin out with about five feet of unwieldy bags piled on the top.
3. Woman's rubbish blows all over the fucking road.
4. It isn't bin day tomorrow.

Saturday December 12th

COVID-19 cases have started to fall. Never fear though. Christmas is around the corner.

Sunday December 13th

I don't like that Rod Liddle a lot, but he's got it right in today's Times. "Test and Trace has cost the taxpayer £22bn. It has repeatedly failed to the achieve targets it has been set. It was once heralded as The Thing That Would Defeat Covid, but nobody talks about it much anymore." So, Dido, by next week I fully expect to see you at the helm of the next taxpayer-funded victory.

First sleep concluded at two of the clock. Danced the mimsy with Juliet until the Mistress made her feelings plain. Summoned Yardley for snuppett, grouse and rowlies, which repast I enjoyed in the scuncheon. After attending His Majesty, penned two letters to Maximillian Tremayne and Sir Lionel Cuffboard regarding a trench. Reprehensible performance of Congreve's "Regard Thy Nothers" at The Royal Court. Then by hog-cart to Tower Hamlets for the exhumation. Carousing at The Harlot's Gurney, where Thom Ridley did eat broken glass until he suffered a dismaying and fatal rectal haemorrhage. And so to bed.

Monday December 14th

There's another COVID-19 variant doing the rounds. That's what they do. Viruses.

We've now seen this year's Town Centre Christmas Tree. It's basically a thirty-foot-tall stick surrounded by confused looking men in Hi-Viz jackets. It's quite festive!

Tuesday December 15th

The two leading medical journals in the UK, the British Medical Journal and the Health Service Journal, stated today that the Government's plans to relax COVID-19 restrictions over Christmas are "a rash decision that could cost many lives". In response to this, Tory politicians quietly muttered that people "might want to stay local".

While we were walking Jack at the park today, we heard the most beautiful birdsong. A few feet from us, perfectly positioned against a brilliant blue sky, was a robin. He sat on his twig proudly singing his incredibly complex tale. You could even see the mist of his little breaths. For five minutes we watched him sing. I have never seen a robin singing up close before. A genuine privilege.

Wednesday December 16th

The Great British Public learned today that the Christmas Jolly is going ahead. God help us.

And you know you're bored when you have a heated debate with your wife about whether dogs have 'minge'.

Thursday December 17th

The conspiracy-theorists have begun to outdo themselves. Little sticky flyers have begun appearing on lamp posts, fences and walls. These look at first glance to be about the Deep State, like the bad comedy getting chalked on the town's pavements. Deep State? Have you seen Boris Johnson lately? He can hardly put his trousers on the right way round. On closer examination, though, they are from an outfit called 'The White Rose'. This Christian organisation cites biblical texts [e.g., The truth will make you free (John 8:32)] as ballast for their arguments that such lifesaving and scientifically proven measures as social distancing, mask-wearing and vaccinations are somehow 'a disgrace to humanity' and 'inhuman and disproportionate'. They have named themselves after a World War II German underground movement called 'Die Weisse Rose'. The leaders of this group were Sophie Scholl, her brother Hans Scholl and their friend Christoph Probst, who all risked their lives by distributing leaflets that called on the people of Germany to resist the Nazi regime. One Weisse Rose leaflet stated that 'every single human is entitled to a government that guarantees the freedom of every single person and the wellbeing of the community'. Nobody can argue with this statement, unless there is something supremely twisted about their world view.

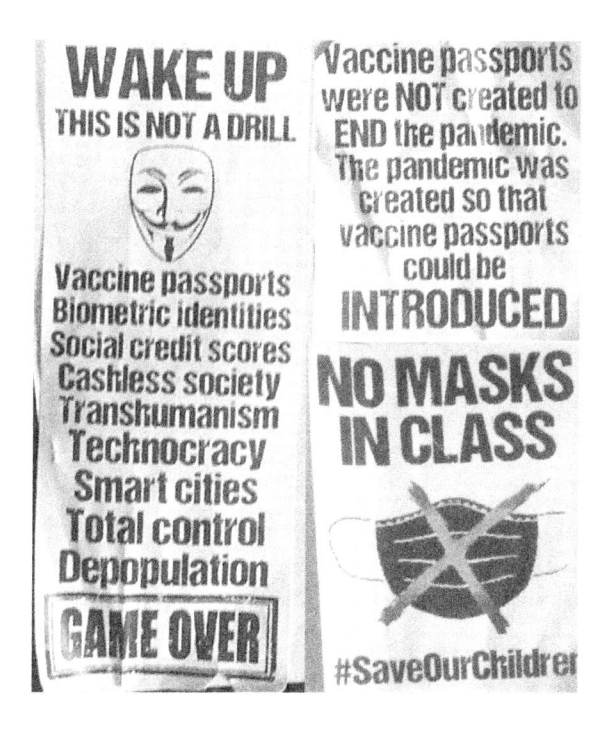

For these ghastly loons to ally themselves with this movement is bad enough. To do so whilst braying their half-arsed and potentially murderous theories is an insult to the very people they are trying so desperately to emulate. In 1943 the Nazis executed Sophie Schloss, Hans Schloss and Christoph Probst in a Munich prison. By guillotine.

Saturday December 19th

Because we're not going anywhere or seeing anyone, unless there is plenty of space available, the new Tier 2/Bubble/Indoor/National/Tier 4/Outdoor/Tier 1/ Rule of Six/Tier 3/Local/Nobody Knows Christmas plans won't affect us in any way. But any poor sods who have made their Christmas plans, however misguidedly, will be totally mystified.

Over two million COVID-19 cases here now.

I came to bed over an hour ago. Wrote the above. Realised I hadn't said goodnight to Linzi. Went back down.

Me: *lengthy romantic goodnight stuff including some hugs and kisses*

Linzi: Fuck off!

Sunday December 20th

Flights from the UK were stopped in Belgium, Canada, France, Germany, Ireland, Italy and The Netherlands today, following the emergence of another new variant of COVID-19. And the Port of Dover is closed.

35,928 new cases of COVID are recorded, almost double the number this time last week.

Monday December 21ˢᵗ

More than forty countries have now suspended flights to and from the UK. I saw a documentary back in the eighties where the UK was described as 'The Dirty Man of Europe'. Plus ça change.

Being dyscalculic, this could be wrong, but I just worked out that if you have just ten sets of three generations (A Grandparent, 80 years old... Their Child, 42... And Their Kid, 20 years old) in a room, you would have enough combined years to go back to 589 A.D, the year that Reccared I, the king of the Visigoths, converted to Catholicism.

Tuesday December 22ⁿᵈ

Now that there's a massive upturn in the latest new variant, UK supermarkets have had to reintroduce a purchasing limit on certain items, including rice, pasta, soap, eggs and, inevitably, toilet roll. This is to ensure that The Great British Public, in their legendary wisdom, empathy and Common Sense, don't empty the bloody shelves. Again.

Wednesday December 23ʳᵈ

This is our usual festive tradition. On December 1ˢᵗ we hang up a felt advent calendar which has little pockets, and we put a chocolate each in the pockets for every day of Advent. With this year being what it's been, we couldn't be bothered with the calendar and just bought a tub of Celebrations, intending to have a sweet each per day. We just did some calculations and estimate, judging by the number of tubs of chocolate we've got through, that today is the 196th of December.

Thursday December 24th (Christmas Eve)

We just found out that something called 'The Christmas Eve Jingle' happened at six o'clock tonight. I looked it up. I'm not certain, but I think we were all supposed to go outside and ring a bell to stop elderly people feeling lonely. If I was an elderly person, lonely or not, and bells suddenly started ringing all over the place, I'd think I was about to enter the hereafter.

I posted not just one but two Christmas videos tonight. One is a version of "Baby It's Cold Outside" that I recorded with my long-time singing companion Lynda, although she did the video, which is two snowmen singing to each other. The second is "Santa Baby", featuring Juliet from The Arguments. The song is great, but I obviously didn't do much filming. And yet again I forgot to properly include the footage we shot in 2019 so the video itself is rubbish. Maybe next year.

Friday December 25th (Christmas Day)

MERRY CHRISTMAS!

My Christmas Day was complete within an hour of waking up. I took Jack out and saw two squirrels sitting on a low branch about eight feet away from me. There they sat, ignoring us, tails twitching, looking at each other. Perched on the branch just up from the squirrels were two lesser spotted woodpeckers. These too had no fear and were carrying on about their business. One of the woodpeckers started doing the Woody Woodpecker pecking thing. It was wonderful. And, in the strangest year ever, things continue to get stranger. There are daffodils and crocuses coming up all over the place. And the tree with the squirrels and woodpeckers has dead brown leaves and new buds on it simultaneously. On Christmas Day. In the morning.

After breakfast I heard from Siiiii's bassist, Ange, who is married to Siiiii's guitarist, Mark. Ange had bought Mark an A-Z of David Bowie podcast that Marc Riley (BBC Radio 6 DJ, late of the much-missed Mark & Lard, The Fall, and Marc Riley & The Creepers) had created, which came on a USB in a little personalised case. When Mark opened his gift this morning, the USB was missing. Disappointed, Ange sent a little email to the chap who had organised the despatch to explain. He replied immediately, promising a replacement. He sent an online link to the podcast by way of consolation. An hour later there was a knock on their door and Marc Riley was standing there with the complete item. What an incredible thing to do at any time of year. On Christmas Morning it's heroic! As ever, Punks are the nicest of people.

We unwrapped what gifts we hadn't already opened after breakfast. Jack made his traditional anti-aircraft flak with the paper. The Antonio Carluccio meal that Linzi creates every year took less time to make because we had pre-prepared some of it. As ever it consisted of an arborio rice, mushroom, spinach, sundried tomato and parmesan stuffed brioche loaf, cranberry and red cabbage, sautéed garlic sprouts and hasselback potatoes.

We received our first ever gift of baked goods from our son and daughter-in-law, and there is much to be said for a tin of fudge and cakes sitting on the coffee table. Not that the fudge and cakes were in it for long. They also gave us some chocolate bars based on that social media meme where the bar names are portmanteau'd. The lads got Tossers, Linzi's a Prick and I got a Cunty bar.

Every Christmas, Linzi buys herself a present. It's an odd concept, but she does it every year. This time she treated herself to something we've called 'Alexa's Mum'. It's an Echo Show and it's like a clever little telly with a powerful speaker. Linzi got it working and we spent most of the day sitting in the living room boozing merrily, requesting festive classics from Alexa's Mum and eating baked goods.

Jack got a toy monkey this year. He always becomes obsessed with his Christmas gift to the point of adoration. The monkey has already started to become a new monotheism. Jack worshipped it initially by trying to chew its head off. Religion, folks. It's that easy!

Best Cracker Joke of the Day:
What's got eight arms and tells the time? A clocktopus!

Just before I gave up on the day's incessant snacking and turned in, I reached that moment where I needed to repeatedly say, "Sorry about the smell". The pickled walnut is surely the unstable incendiary grenade of Christmas treats.

Saturday December 26th (Boxing Day)

One of my favourite parts of Christmas is the Boxing Day Bubble & Squeak Breakfast. It's basically everything nobody ate yesterday chucked in a skillet, fried to a crisp and eaten with fried eggs and brown sauce. I get it all to myself too, as everyone else thinks it's revolting. It's the only bubble I'm going anywhere near at any rate.

Boxing Day also means it's my day to cook. This year's offering was a Quorn Family Roast, creamed potatoes, carrots, sprouts, peas, leeks in mature cheddar and Parmesan sauce, honey roast parsnips, Delia Smith roast Maris Pipers and redcurrant gravy.

Afterwards we collapsed.

I liked today. Apart from dinner-timings I didn't need to engage my brain once.

Sunday December 27th

Today started with a surprise post-Boxing Day Bubble & Squeak. Lovely old job!

More good news from clever people too! AstraZeneca say that the Oxford/AstraZeneca vaccine is a "winning formula". And it looks like it will be available within days.

Meanwhile, in Australia, they have found the B117 strain of COVID-19. This is the variant that made British people start hoarding bogroll again.

Monday December 28th

Another 41,385 COVID-19 cases were recorded in the UK today. Officials have "expressed concern" about the NHS. It's a shame that these 'officials' didn't think about that before they encouraged everyone to go on a hoolie for Christmas.

The upmarket Swiss ski resort of Verbier witnessed about 300 opulent British tourists frantically trying to get home before it impacted their precious little lives too much, after Switzerland imposed a retrospective ten-day quarantine backdated to 14th December because of that pesky B117 strain.

Tuesday December 29th

There are more of those Tiers announced today. I don't understand. Nobody understands. The 2021 New Year Honours List was published today. Hundreds of people are being honoured for their efforts during the last year. Hancock warns people not to get together for New Year. Oh Matt. You're such a fucking idiot. 55,892 new COVID-19 cases today, which is the most ever. The year is nearly done. We made it. I keep thinking about the thousands who didn't.

Tonight we're drinking Advokaat. It's like festive Gaviscon.

Thursday December 31st (New Year's Eve)

At midnight tonight, the world is going to look into the frozen sky and witness two grim giants battle for supremacy, their vast stony faces impassive, as dreadful 2021 roars its victory over the prone and hideous carcass of 2020.

We drank Scotch and snowballs and wine and watched the TV.

HAPPY NEW YEAR!

21 WEEKS IN 2021

January

Jack was Thirteen: Once more we both had to wait for our Large Haddock and Chips.

Second Wave & Lockdown III: Nurses wept. Doctors were in pieces. People were still dying terrible deaths. The Government was still smirking and taking credit for doing nothing.

Vaccines Began Nationwide Rollout: Thanks to the NHS.

Violent Trump Supporters Stormed US Capitol: Resulting in five deaths and the evacuation of the building. All of this after a rabble-rousing speech by Trump.

Biden and Harris Inaugurated: 20,000 troops were authorised to guard Washington D.C. on the day. This was more than all those stationed in Afghanistan, Iraq, Syria and Somalia. Joe Biden is the 46th President. Kamala Harris is the first female, black and Asian Vice President in history. Lady Gaga sang. Amanda Gorman beautifully recited "The Hill We Climb". We watched. I cried. It was beautiful. Biden immediately signed fifteen executive orders to re-join the WHO, the Paris Climate Agreement, revoking the Keystone XL Pipeline and making face-coverings mandatory on US federal properties.

Facebook and Twitter Blocked Trump: For Incitement to Violence.

45,000-Year-Old Cave Painting Discovered: It's a pig!

Cremation Disappointment: I went right through my Pure Cremation literature and there was absolutely no option to have the procedure filmed so my loved ones can see exactly when I'm 'done to a turn'.

Weather: Bloody freezing, but it was January.

February

Joe Biden Kept Signing Executive Orders: To reunite immigrant families and to set up a new force to address around a thousand separated families.

The Back of My Car is Alive: I discovered that I can stand upright and shelter from the rain beneath the open tailgate of our car. While I was there, I examined the area where the tailgate sits when closed. It hasn't had a clean for about six years, and I thought I would come up with one word to describe it. That word is "ecosystem".

Trump Impeachment: Began in Washington D.C. I was rooting for the Death Penalty. By garrotting if possible. Or flaying. Anything really.

UK Kent COVID-19 Variant: It started to sweep the world and became the dominant strain globally.

'Lockdown' Or Is It?: An incredible volume of daily traffic. Drywall vans. Carwash maintenance vans. Scaffolders. Carpet fitters. Mobile beauticians. Gym equipment maintenance. And so on. There was no lockdown. This was like having a hospital isolation ward in the middle of the canteen.

Trump Acquitted: Thanks to the spineless GOP.

Litter Picking: Performed my first litter pick. Filled a very large gardening sack with hundreds of bits of random plastic, cider tins, carrier bags, lager bottles, shed components and what looked like half a car dashboard.

12 String Guitar: Sold it. It was just taking up space.

Aggressive Hedgers: I took Jack out. I stood on the main road opposite their house. Mr Hedger was messing about with their minging van. I started loudly whistling "The Marrow Song". He took one look at me standing there with Jack. Then he ran away into their house like a fucking greyhound.

Disneycore: I decided to invent a brand-new post-punk genre.

Another Sigmoidoscopy: Clean bill of health. I asked the consultant what the problem might have been. She said I might have nicked my bum with something. She didn't expand on what that may have been. She also said that I have quite a 'Craggy Bottom' and that a 'Crag' may have become a bit too 'Craggy'.

Weather: Bloody freezing or raining.

March

NHS Nurses: After all the clapping and praise, the mealy-mouthed Tory Government gifted them a 1% pay increase.

Oprah Winfrey: On March 7th, she interviewed Harry and Meghan, Duke and Duchess of Sussex. The interview was broadcast on CBS. Meghan says that she had been suicidal and that she was subject to racism from the Royal Family.

Piers Morgan: Stormed out of the Good Morning Britain studio two days later after being held to account, in the light of Black Lives Matter, by weather presenter Alex Beresford, for saying he "didn't believe a word of it."

Equilibrium was finally restored in that I could comfortably loath the bloke again.

Covid Jab: We had our vaccinations together the day before Mother's Day. Linzi went to bed, and I felt increasingly poorly the next day, but needed to take care of the dog and the house before I keeled over. My iPad bonged at about 3pm and my actual mother was leering out of the screen at me on FaceTime for the first time ever. I jumped out of my skin. Horrible feverish night, but not as bad as the flu jab last year.

Declassified US Intelligence Report: Finds that Putin authorised efforts to aid re-election of Trump.

ITV: Broadcast an item about milking horses.

COVID-19: People were still dying. Government were still a barrowload of shit.

India: 47,262 cases of a new 'Indian Variant' were reported.

Weather: Bloody freezing or raining all the time.

April

Easter Weekend: Hundreds of tons of rubbish was left on beaches and in beauty spots and parks. I wish these TV talking heads would stop saying it's 'a small minority' of people doing this. Hundreds of tons of litter is not the work of a 'small minority'. People are skanks.

Low Carb Again: Because I was worth it. And I was fat.

Prince Philip, The Duke of Edinburgh: Died on April 9th.

Prince Philip, The Duke of Edinburgh: Still dead on April 11th. Many of those not directly bereaved were asking "where can I find something decent on the telly?"

India: People were dying of COVID-19 in the streets. Hospitals were overflowing. Smoke from funeral pyres blackened the sky. Supplies of medicines and oxygen were running out. It was apocalyptic.

Pakistan and Bangladesh: Due to soaring virus infections, Pakistan and Bangladesh were on the UK's 'Red List' for incoming travel. India was not, although the number of cases there dwarfed those in the other two countries.

Disneycore: Linzi and I collaborated on our first song recording, called The Hearse Song. Linzi watched the video once and said, "I don't need to see that again." It's about human decomposition. In a coffin.

Chauvin Found Guilty: Ex-Minnesota police officer Derek Chauvin was found guilty of murdering George Floyd on all three counts by a jury on April 20th. Every decent human being on the planet applauded.

Lyrid Meteor Shower: I intended to take my astral binoculars out to watch these. Then I found out that they're in the tail of something called the 'Thatcher Comet'. So they can fuck off.

B.1.617: This is the 'Indian Variant'. And it's starting to appear in the UK.

Travel Ban: India was finally added to the Red List on April 23rd.

Pints of Beer: Following Beer Garden Restriction lifting, we had our first pint at Beckets Inn for months. The garden looked stunning. We had a lovely chat with Brigid, and I signed her copy of The Devine Comedy. It was almost like old times. All socially distanced and masked though. And the new Marston's beers were lush. Neither of us had ever left a pub feeling elated before.

Weather: Bloody freezing and raining all the bastard time.

May

Happy Beltane: We did not witness the frigid Sun rising like an iceberg over the chilly wastes of the Somerset Tundra today. Maybe next year, COVID-19 variants and permafrost permitting.

Low Carb: The Low Carb was working. I have two barometers when it comes to weight loss, as I don't weigh myself. The first is: Can I see my seatbelt while I'm driving? It was a bit early for that. The second is: Can I see my willy while I'm having a wee? And I could! Clearly! In February I couldn't see the fucking toilet.

Tory Election Landslide: The Tories had a brilliant night because the NHS have been superb at delivering vaccines, despite being run into the ground by the Tories. At the Hartlepool by-election, Jill Mortimer became the first Conservative MP since 1974. A Hartlepool representative of the Great British Public, when asked why he voted for the Conservatives, said it was because the Tories had given the town more Food Banks than Labour.

Naked Gardening Day 2021:

Indian Variant: Johnson says he will send in the Army to Indian Variant hotspots in the UK, which are mainly in Yorkshire and the Humber, in Northern England. It is feared that this variant is up to 50% more transmissible than the Kent Variant and that the vaccines may not be as effective. 294 people with this variant went untraced for three weeks. Perhaps the Government 'missed the email' again.

Restrictions Lift: On May 17th COVID-19 restrictions were lifted further. Up to six people from three households could now meet in indoor public places like pubs. Up to eight people from eight households could meet anywhere outdoors, and kids under twelve weren't counted. Or they were. Or something. God knows.

Spouting Shit Like Trump: Environment Secretary George Eustace was on the telly explaining why it took so long to put India on the Red List. He said that India didn't have high COVID-19 levels because there was a high level of COVID-19 in India. It was because India was carrying out more tests.

Travel Traffic Lights: There were three. Red, Amber and Green. Johnson said that Red was 'Do Not Go', Amber was 'Go, But Quarantine Afterwards', and Green was 'Go On, What are You Waiting For!'. Once thousands of British people began flocking to Amber countries, he changed that to: Amber also means 'Go, But Only If A Relative There Is About to Die'.

Travel Wealth Apartheid: Because the cost of testing on arriving back from holiday destinations were enormous (£65 to £200 per PCR test), many people would be paying more on the COVID-19 tests they were legally obliged to take than their holidays. These UK tests are twice as costly as on the European mainland. Ah, the Sunny Uplands of Brexit Britain. Where the oiks can watch the jets flying overhead from a whelk stall in Skegness.

Conservative Islamophobia: The UK's Equality and Human Rights Commission found that most discrimination within the Tory party relates to anti-Muslim racism and singled out Johnson for his previous comments about 'letterboxes' and 'bankrobbers'. Johnson made a statement to the effect that "I may have used this language in the past, but now I am PM I would not." So what? I used live in Helions Bumpstead and I used to be a drainage engineer and I have *never* used this language.

Dominic Cummings: On May 26th, in front of a live, televised, seven-hour joint session of the Commons Health, and Science and Technology committee, Cummings made statements about his time in Number 10 during the ongoing COVID-19 Pandemic.

Amongst other fireworks, Cummings lit the blue touchpaper under:

The first 'lockdown' was too late.
Hancock 'should have been fired' about twenty times, and he's also a bloody liar.
Johnson was unfit for office, and he didn't want a second 'lockdown'.
Johnson wanted Chris Whitty to inject him with COVID-19 live on TV.
Thousands of people died needlessly from COVID-19.
There was no Ring of Steel around Care Homes. There was nothing.
Johnson thought the virus was a scare story.
The Government continuously failed.

Naturally, Johnson, Hancock and his pals said Who, Me? and we were back to the Infallible British Gods scenario. Johnson made a typically blustering statement in the Commons, demonstrating both his Tin Ear and his contempt for front line NHS staff and bereaved families who concurred with Cummings. I am in no way a Dominic Cummings fan, but if he was lying he's the most gifted liar I have witnessed in my entire life.

Unintentionally Hilarious White Rose Anti-COVID-19 Restriction Sticker: "Of Course Cases Are Going Up. They Are Doing More Tests! If They Did More IQ Tests, IQ's Would Go Up! Idiot!!" I tried to take it down to keep, but unfortunately it tore in half.

Marcus Rashford MBE: The Manchester United and England forward received more than seventy online racial slurs following a game in Gdansk on May 26th. Some of these were from a British teacher. Marcus Rashford has raised both money and the profile of child poverty in the

UK and beyond. He forced Johnson's sadistic regime to do a U-Turn on free school meals for poor kids, and he has worked for fairness in Universal Credit and the increase of literacy. He doesn't need to do any of this. But he is a good person so he does. Because he is black, the abuse is rife If anyone thinks Black Lives Matter became redundant after the sentencing of Derek Chauvin, they are woefully naïve. Racism, by its nature, is the realm of very stupid people. It is also the domain of the Scum of The Earth.

Cloud Dream: May was a month for disturbed sleep. On May 26th I had a vivid and sanity destroying dream. In this nightmare, Cloud had somehow survived her euthanasia. They had got it all wrong. The lethal injection had not worked, and she regained consciousness on the way to the Pet Crematorium. The driver heard her and let her out of the van. In my dream she spent three years trying to get home. Our road, meanwhile, had become derelict and abandoned. I eventually found out about her survival and spent months trying to find her. She hid, scared, in the ruins of her old garden and waiting for us to return for years. When I finally came back here, to our old, abandoned home, she didn't know who I was. Then she recognised me and, aged and crippled, came towards me. I took her into my arms. She licked me once. Then her body went limp as she died.

Bank Holiday Ahoy: Skips, Environmental Health Officers and Refuse Contractors at the ready, UK Councils!

Weather: Bloody freezing and raining all the bastard time until the 25th. Then it was lovely.

AFTERWORD

What have we learned from this strangest of years? The politicians, by and large, will have learned nothing. They never do, because they never need to. They will be safe from too much sticky criticism, at least in this country. Their gravy train is impermeable. For centuries these people have lied and played fast-and-loose with the truth. Although Cummings has now chucked in a curver.

The NHS, we can hope, will cease to be an economic punchbag simply because it is full of people who care, and will instead become cherished again. Supermarket staff. Delivery drivers. Recycling operatives. Postal workers. Teachers. They are all now understood to be Front Line Workers, along with the NHS and the Emergency Services. And they should continue to be valued in this way. We clapped for all these Heroes every Thursday. For a while anyway.

To begin with, there was a strange ethereal melancholy about the novelty of living within the construct of a Hollywood disaster movie. Our human noise dwindled. The birds sang louder. We could hear the wind. Contrails vanished. The sun shone. The air became pristine. Cars disappeared from the roads and, at night, the streets were silent. There was an unspoken understanding that we were, genuinely for once, all in this together. Partly, I suspect, this spirit was because nobody knew what was going on. The marching necklace of stars in that warm long-ago March sky defined this moment in time. The stillness. The strangeness. The almost tangible mutual love our species is capable of when we are confronted by the utterly unknown. Then, as the year ran ahead of us, that all changed.

As with Brexit, people got bored with what, in part, their own behaviour was causing. Our sole trip to the local shopping village was proof of that. The inability to adhere to safeguards put in place by the retailers. The disregard for others. It was palpable and frightening. Besides the trolley vote-test, this most familiar object can be a gauge for more general public behaviours. When they have shopped, many people just leave their trolley where it is. It's the legendary *'someone else will do it'*. Why spend fifteen seconds of your valuable time doing the right thing when you can dump it in a parking bay? A similar phenomenon is streams of cars refusing to slow down for a moment to allow the person pulling out of a junction to carry on with their journey. It's dull selfishness and it's everywhere. The Government didn't help the situation either, of course. Giving confusing and contradictory messages at every turn. Attempting to keep our taxes a-rolling in while simultaneously giving health advice was doomed from the very start. Because it was impossible. And the Care Home fiasco back in March showed the Tories in their truest light.

When people ask us what we did during the Great Covid-19 Pandemic of 2020, I wonder how we will respond. Did we help the situation? Did we think of anyone but ourselves and those within our "bubbles"? Did we blindly adhere to the agendas of those in power, their eyes focused on The Bottom Line as ever? Did we Socially Distance for safety's sake? Or did we watch box-sets and then meander through our lives with total disregard for other people? Did we understand that a person's worth isn't dependent upon who they are or what they have, but rather on what they do? Did we choose to explain something we couldn't understand by concocting ridiculous Illuminati or The Deep State conspiracies? I only saw one missive by these people that made any sense. It was stuck to a lamp post and asked "Do You Think the Government Cares About You?" Well, no. But neither do viruses. And, apart from the ballot box and science, there is very little to be done about either problem. And that isn't the point anyway. It never was. The point, throughout the whole of this, has been "Did We Care About Each Other?"

The baton of care was passed. From the NHS. From Black Lives Matter. From Amazon Drivers. From carers. From the clever people who nearly killed themselves finding vaccines for the world. From Captain Sir Tom Moore. From the little kids who emulated him. From the supermarket staff. From everyone who thought of other people. And who was the baton passed to? And did we care in return?

I sincerely hope we did, or at least that we tried. It is ridiculous to believe that COVID-19 is Operation Last Gasp for viruses. The pandemic isn't even over yet. And even if we do vanquish or learn to live with COVID-19, there are thousands of others waiting around the corner. Nipah, Zika, Lassa Fever, Monkeypox (I may call my next solo album Monkeypox if I ever finish it), Ebola…

Whatever it is, and whenever it strikes, we need to remember what is important. What isn't important is the acquisition of vast wealth. Or power. Or plaudits. Or social-standing. Viruses are one of the few organisms, at least in Britain, that *really* don't care where your father went to school or how much wealth you have. The important thing about life is, as it has always been, loving and caring. For everyone.

ACKNOWLEDGEMENTS & THANKS

To the NHS and all Frontline Workers for everything.

To Linzi for putting up with my tip-tapping away on this keyboard while she's watching the TV, and for being generally very fine.

To Jack for being great diary-fodder.

To K&L for K&S.

To Loki for the great artistic and digital assistance.

To Fi for the sleep.

To Mia for the Wisdom.

To Howard Gardner for the Thomas cross-section.

To Michael Green for the inspiration.

In closing, for those who think that writing books is easy, as I did once upon a time, I present my book-writing workstation.

It's a dog.

GOODBYE

Printed in Great Britain
by Amazon